"Can we talk about the rules for a minute?" he asked.

"Rules?"

He waved his hand. "Expectations. Firm expectations. We remain in visual contact at all times. That means you don't even step outside for a quick breath of fresh air without me. If you have to go to the bathroom, I'll check it first and then stand outside the door."

"I know we're supposed to be newlyweds, but won't people think that's just a little over the top?"

"I'll do it in a way that people won't even notice."

She thought he perhaps underestimated that every woman's eyes in the place would follow him. He was just so darn handsome, so darn male. "Got it. Visual contact. At all times. It's just that I'm a little disappointed."

"Why?" He looked very concerned.

She lowered her lashes. "Well, Detective Hollister. That wasn't the only kind of contact I was hoping for tonight."

HIDDEN WITNESS

—

BEVERLY LONG

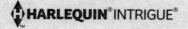

HARLEQUIN® INTRIGUE®

For Kate, Nick and Lydia,
who have a wonderful new home in Missouri.

Recycling programs
for this product may
not exist in your area.

ISBN-13: 978-0-373-74925-6

Hidden Witness

Copyright © 2015 by Beverly R. Long

Printed in U.S.A.

www.Harlequin.com

Beverly Long enjoys the opportunity to write her own stories. She has both a bachelor's and a master's degree in business and more than twenty years of experience as a human resources director. She considers her books to be a great success if they compel the reader to stay up way past their bedtime. Beverly loves to hear from readers. Visit beverlylong.com, or like her at facebook.com/beverlylong.romance.

Books by Beverly Long

Harlequin Intrigue

Return to Ravesville

Hidden Witness

The Men from Crow Hollow

Hunted
Stalked
Trapped

The Detectives

Deadly Force
Secure Location

Visit the Author Profile page at
Harlequin.com for more titles.

CAST OF CHARACTERS

Chase Hollister—He's a seasoned St. Louis police detective, but suddenly he's babysitting a witness in Ravesville, Missouri, at his family's homestead, a place he never intended to return to.

Raney Taylor—She's willing to testify against serial killer Harry Malone, but somebody seems determined to make sure she doesn't. Can she trust Detective Hollister to keep her safe?

Harry Malone—He made a mistake in underestimating Raney Taylor. But even from behind bars, he may be orchestrating a hit on Raney in order to finish what he started.

Luis Vincenze—He's a Florida cop, assigned to deliver Raney to Missouri. Is Raney's trust in him misplaced? Who is he really working for?

Lloyd Doogan—He has an explanation for why he attacks Raney, but can Chase truly trust a man who has Brick Doogan's blood?

Dawson Roy—He's Chase's partner and one of the few who knows where Chase and Raney are hiding. Is it possible that he'd have sold them out?

Gary Blake—Is he merely a lazy cop, or is he hiding a much bigger secret?

Sheila Stanton—She wants to pick up where she and Chase left off more than a decade earlier. But would she go so far as to harm Raney?

Chapter One

Chase Hollister heard his cell phone ring and used his forearm to pull the pillow that he slept half-on and half-under closer around his ears. It rang four times and clicked over to voice mail. Thirty seconds later, it started ringing again.

"Damn," he muttered, tossing off the pillow. He glanced at the number, saw that it was his brother and reached for the phone.

He pushed a button. "I have not had any sleep for twenty-eight hours," Chase said. "This better be good."

"Brick is dead," Bray said.

Chase sat up in bed. He hadn't heard the man's name in over eight years. Hadn't spoken it himself for much longer. "How?"

"Car accident. His sister was with him. They had a double funeral two days ago."

Chase had met his stepfather's older sister once, maybe twice. He recalled that even as a teenager, he'd known there was something odd about her. That family had a bad gene pool.

"Anybody else get hurt?" Chase asked.

"Nope. One car. Only Brick and Adelle in it. They were on their way to Brick's doctor's appointment."

He lay back down. He didn't care about the details. "I'm going back to bed."

"I got a call from Mom's attorney," Bray said. "The house is ours."

In one smooth movement, Chase swung his body out of bed. His bare feet hit the soft rug first, then the polished hardwood. He walked down the short hallway and into his kitchen. The blinds were up and he was naked. He didn't care. He needed coffee. "That doesn't make sense. Brick had a son. I assume the man is still alive."

"I'm not sure but it's a moot point. When Mom died eight years ago, the house was in a trust for us. Brick had been granted lifetime use. The attorney said that we should have been made aware of that upon Mom's death but it was a slipup."

The irony was not lost on Chase. They could have fought the lifetime-use thing and booted him out of there. He'd have been on the outside looking in, kind of like Chase had been whenever Brick got a wild hair and locked him out.

He dumped some coffee in a filter, poured water in the coffeepot and flipped the start button. He didn't put the pot on the burner. Instead, he held a cup directly under the streaming coffee.

"You've got to go there and see what we need to do to get rid of the place," Bray said.

Chase jiggled the cup and hot liquid burned his hand. "No way," he said. "You go, you're the oldest."

"I would if I could. I'm three weeks into a new assignment. I can't pull out now."

"Cal will have to do it. We're older, we can make him." Chase added the familiar taunt, knowing there was nothing easy or familiar about his relationship with Cal.

"He's out of the country."

Cal had spent most of the past eight years out of the country. That was what navy SEALs did. For the past six months, following his discharge, he'd been working as a contractor. That was what his business card said. Chase supposed it could be true if the new breed of contractor was trained to blow up the bad guys, disarm bombs and generally screw with the enemy. "Well, I don't care if he's on the moon. I'm busy, too, you know. I've only been back for a week."

"How is the leg?"

Functional. Still not up to full strength.
"Fine," Chase said.

"I thought you were going to be out for six weeks," Bray prodded. "You went back at four."

"We're short staffed."

"Aren't we all? I was especially impressed when your name popped up on one of my search engines. Then, when I dug a little deeper, I realized you were busy being a hero on your second day back."

Chase didn't answer. He'd hated the photo, the article, the attention. Hadn't considered that it went beyond the print edition.

"'Detective Chase Hollister, one of St. Louis's finest, keeping the streets safe for the rest of us,'" Bray recited.

His brother did his own part to keep the streets safe. Working undercover for the DEA wasn't easy. He would have hated the attention, too. But now he was picking a fight in hopes that Chase, wanting to end the conversation, would agree to take care of things. It wasn't going to work.

"Listen, Bray. It's simple. I'm not going back. The house can rot for all I care," he said. Chase hung up and tossed his cell phone onto the granite countertop. The noise echoed through the quiet apartment. Then he stood in his stainless-steel kitchen and sipped his coffee, burning his tongue in the process.

Ravesville, Missouri. Two hours southwest of St. Louis. A little town in the middle of the country, undisturbed by major highways and big box stores. A place where everybody knew their neighbor, talked about them freely and dropped everything when they needed a hand. It was the kind of place where a kid got on his bike at eight o'clock on a summer morning and didn't come home until dinner. The kind of place where there were community-wide chili dinners and pancake breakfasts and people stuck around to clear the tables and wash the dirty dishes. It had been home. And he'd been a happy enough kid.

And then everything had changed the summer his dad died. Chase had been fourteen, just about to enter high school. And as bad as his dying had been, it had gotten worse two years later when his mother had remarried and Brick had become his stepfather.

There probably wasn't a meaner man in the entire state. Why he'd married a woman with three teenage boys when he didn't appear to like kids was a mystery. He was estranged from his own son, who was quite a bit older than the Hollister boys. Chase could only remember meeting him once.

When the phone rang again less than five minutes later, he picked it up, ready to give his brother an earful. At the last second, he realized it was his partner's number. The man should have been sleeping, too. He'd been awake the same twenty-eight hours.

"Yeah," Chase said.

"The boss called. He just heard from the chief," Dawson said. "Somebody used the Florida witness in the Malone case for target practice."

He and Dawson hadn't worked the Malone case but the man was suspected of murdering three Missouri women about a year ago, one of whom was the chief's godchild. Harry Malone was currently locked up in the county jail awaiting trial and everybody in the St. Louis Police Department, from the janitor up, had an interest in the case. "That doesn't make sense. That woman should have been sealed up tighter than your wallet."

"Funny."

"Was she injured?"

"No. Lorraine Taylor got lucky."

Then, it was the second time she'd gotten lucky. He wasn't sure of the details but through the grapevine he'd heard that she'd somehow managed to get away from Harry Malone. She'd told the cops about the pictures of the dead women that Harry Malone had proudly shown her and the admission Malone had made about killing the women. She'd been able to lead them back to the apartment where she'd been held. Unfortunately, by that time, Harry and his pictures were gone. But her DNA had been in several places in the apartment and she'd had injuries consistent with her story.

But Harry had been careful and there was no physical evidence linking him to the Missouri murders because there were no bodies.

Even so, based on the information that Lorraine Taylor had provided, Harry Malone had been picked up and charged with kidnapping and assorted other crimes and three counts of murder. Lorraine Taylor had likely assumed that she'd done her civic duty by leading the police to the man and that she could get on with her life.

However, she'd no doubt quickly reevaluated those plans six weeks later after almost being killed by a hit-and-run as she walked to work. Witnesses had substantiated that the attack was deliberate. That was where it got complicated. Following her escape from Malone, Lorraine Taylor's identity had been closely guarded and her name had never made the newspapers.

Unfortunately, in the information age, that didn't mean much. Cops in both Florida and

St. Louis knew her name. Then there were the people in the prosecuting attorney's office and the judge's office. Harry Malone certainly knew who she was, and jail might impede communication with the outside world but it certainly didn't stop it.

The cops considered whether the attack on Taylor could have been unrelated to her potential testimony against Malone. But even if that was true, it didn't really matter. Any attack, for whatever reason, had the potential of robbing the State of Missouri of their prime witness.

They'd decided to put her in a safe house. That was the last that Chase had heard.

Now somebody had shot at her. That was going to make a lot of people nervous, people who were counting on the fact that Lorraine Taylor was going to be an excellent witness.

She was going to have to be. Harry Malone, a rich, second-generation hedge-fund trader from New York, wasn't stupid. He wasn't talking and he'd retained a very good defense attorney. He'd been deemed a flight risk and denied bail so his attorney was working expeditiously to get the trial under way.

Plus, the scuttlebutt was that Malone was confident that he was going to walk free.

Was it possible that he wasn't as confident as he wanted others to believe and he'd decided to ensure his freedom by getting rid of Lorraine Taylor?

"The chief wants her moved to St. Louis," Dawson said.

The chief was a known control freak and, given his personal interest in this case, there was probably no talking him out of it. But Chase understood. They needed Lorraine Taylor.

"He told the boss that he wants us to start working on it," Dawson said.

"Why us?" They weren't the most senior detectives on the force. He'd barely spoken ten words to the chief and he figured it was the same for Dawson. He didn't care; brown-nosing his way to the top wasn't his style. Besides, who knew how long he was going to stick around? Maybe there was a better job around the corner.

"According to the boss, the chief said that we did a hell of a job in the Brodger case."

Hamas Brodger had been a drug dealer who had executed three teenage boys who'd tried to screw him out of a couple hundred dollars. A fourth boy had managed to get away. Chase and Dawson had babysat him, twelve-on, twelve-off, for six weeks. It hadn't been a good assignment. The kid didn't bathe regularly and had forgotten all the manners he'd learned in kindergarten. And he hadn't been able to keep his fingers away from social media and had led the bad guys to their door. Chase had taken a bullet in the leg as a result but had managed to get his own shot off.

The kid had testified and Brodger was going to call the state penitentiary home for a long time.

"I think you maybe should have let the guy shoot him," Dawson said. "The way it turned out, it's just getting us more work."

"Maybe next time," Chase said. "But listen, I may need to take a day off pretty soon. I've… uh… I've got something I need to take care of. Family business."

"Your brothers okay?" Dawson asked, his tone serious.

"Yeah. They're fine. My stepfather just died."

Dawson didn't offer the normal platitudes. He didn't know everything but he knew enough. "Can I help?" he asked.

"Nope. Just got to take care of a house. The lieutenant doesn't expect us back in, does he?"

"He said tomorrow was soon enough. Lorraine Taylor will be here then. The question is, what are we going to do with her?"

RANEY TAYLOR WAS FURIOUS. The nightmare that had started the evening Harry Malone had wandered into Next Steps and volunteered to help was never going to end.

Wasn't it enough that she was going to have to testify and relive every awful moment of the fifty-four hours that she spent with him? As horrible as that would be, she knew she had to do it. The man had to be stopped.

Once he'd been arrested, it had never occurred to her that she would still be in danger. She'd gone back to work, brushed aside the comments from coworkers that she really should take more time off and hoped that someday, she'd be able to trust again. And each day had gotten a little easier. But six weeks later, when a dark SUV had tried to run her down three blocks from her house, she'd realized that things were about to get a lot harder.

The police had promised that they could keep her safe. *Don't worry*, they'd said, handing her the keys to the two-bedroom house in the modest Miami neighborhood. *We keep witnesses here all the time. Nothing ever happens.* Now they were going to have to change their sales pitch because last night, eleven days after moving in, someone had taken a shot at her as she took the garbage to the curb.

If she hadn't bent down to chase a wayward napkin, she'd be dead right now.

She'd assumed she'd be moved to another

place. She hadn't expected them to announce that she needed to pack quickly because she was getting on a plane. And going to St. Louis.

She'd known that at some point she'd have to travel to the Midwestern city. Harry Malone's trial was taking place there because his three other victims had all resided in Missouri.

She'd never met the other victims but she *knew* them. Could easily imagine the terror they'd lived through. After her escape, she hadn't been able to keep from looking up the news stories. Had wanted to see the women as people, had wanted to know they had lives and that they'd been loved. Had needed to replace the images she carried in her head with something else.

She did not want to be in the same city with Malone. She'd made a terrible mistake in trusting him. And had almost paid the ultimate price.

She rubbed her ribs. He'd cracked three of them with a well-placed kick after he'd dumped her blindfolded on the floor of his squalid apartment. The doctor had told her that the bones would knit back together quickly but it might take months for the bruising to heal. Every night when she rolled over in bed, it woke her up.

Not that she was sleeping a whole lot anyway.

Maybe that would change in St. Louis. Maybe she could sleep away the next month until she had to testify at the trial. Leaving her job pained her more than anything. She loved her work.

Her clients, most of whom came from disadvantaged circumstances, wanted to work but for one reason or another had trouble securing employment. The assistance she provided took many forms. She taught basic communication skills to some. Took others shopping so that they understood what to wear to work. She'd helped with table manners, organizational skills and conflict management.

It made her day when a client showed up with his or her first paycheck. It made her week when they were still working at that same job three months later. She was over the moon when they celebrated their first anniversary.

Now Harry Malone had taken that away from her. That and more.

She jumped when there was a light tap at the door. "Ready, Ms. Taylor?" the officer asked. Luis had been with her since day one of her *captivity* and he'd been unfailingly polite.

"I don't understand why I have to go to St. Louis," she said for the twentieth time. "This is a big city, a big state. Surely you have other safe houses."

The older man shrugged. "All I know is that you need to be on the nine-fifteen flight to St. Louis. Maybe it won't be as hot there."

In late September, Miami was still stifling hot. Not that she'd been outside much lately. It would be wonderful if they stashed her someplace where she had access to a balcony or a porch.

"Fine. Let's just get this over with," she said.

CHASE MET DAWSON in the front lobby of police headquarters and they rode the elevator in silence. "How's Mary?" Chase asked as the doors opened.

"She said her ankles have swelled to the size of cantaloupes and her back feels as if a small army of angry men with sharp knives have taken residence."

"Damn. Want to stay at my place for a few days?"

Dawson shook his head. "I'd have to stay thirty-six days, and if I did that, I don't think I'd have a happy home to return to once the little princess is born."

Chase pulled open the heavy door that led them to the interior office. "I don't like coming here," he whispered.

Dawson shrugged. "Then, quit doing crazy things that get you noticed by the top brass."

"I don't do crazy things," he denied.

"Five weeks ago, you took a bullet in your thigh and still managed to return fire. You pushed your recovery, got the doc to release you early and came back to work last week. A day later, you walked through a wall of fire. And it was all caught on a cell phone. The newspaper called you a hero and the video played on the evening news—both the six o'clock and the ten o'clock," he said. "And you hadn't even clocked in for the day," he added, sounding exasperated.

It had been early and the two young men had been drag racing on their way to work. He'd just gotten the first guy out of his car when the second car had exploded, potentially trapping the young driver. "You wouldn't have left that kid to die."

Dawson smiled at the young woman behind the desk. "Detectives Roy and Hollister here to see Chief Bates." When she picked up the phone, he turned to Chase. "I wouldn't have wanted to," he said, his tone serious. "But I'm not sure I'd have had the guts to do what you did," he added. "You had to have been concerned that your leg might not hold up."

He'd considered the possibility. Then ignored it. Those kids were going to have a future. That was what mattered.

The chief only made them wait ten minutes. When they were ushered into his office, Chase was again reminded that Chief Bates was one tough dude. While he was close to sixty, he was six-five, with a barrel chest and a handshake that could bring a man to his knees.

He extended his arm to Dawson. "Detective Roy," he said. "Good to see you." He turned toward Chase. "Detective Hollister. How's the leg?"

"Fine."

The chief nodded. "Saw you on the news the other day. Nice work."

Behind the chief, Dawson made a big deal out of rolling his eyes. Chase ignored him.

"Sit, please," the chief said, pointing to the leather chairs in front of his big cherry desk. "You know what our situation is?"

Chase nodded. "There was a second attempt on Lorraine Taylor's life."

"Yes. Malone has access to considerable resources. It's possible that he managed to organize a hit on her before the Florida police got him picked up. It's also possible that he did it from jail."

The words lingered in the air. Good cops hated that there were dirty cops but it was a fact of life. Palms got greased and instructions often made it over the prison wall. Or maybe it had been a visitor who carried messages back and forth. The possibilities really were endless.

Chase leaned forward in his chair. "Could Malone have had an accomplice? Somebody who knew Lorraine Taylor. Knew her because it wasn't an accident that she was the victim. Maybe she was cherry-picked and when things went badly for Malone and he was picked up, the accomplice slipped into action?"

"It's possible. But Taylor didn't see anybody else while she was with Malone or hear him refer to anyone."

But Malone was smart—nobody was disputing that. He'd managed to kill three women and hide their bodies.

The chief steepled his big fingers together. "It's even possible that we've got some crackpot who somehow managed to find out Taylor's identity and he or she has decided to finish what Malone started."

Chase nodded. "I guess the only thing we really know for sure is that we need to keep Lorraine Taylor alive to testify at Harry Malone's trial."

"Alive and unintimidated," the chief corrected. "I'm worried that she's not going to be a good witness if she's frightened that her life is in danger. We need her confident. Relaxed," he added, then had the wherewithal to look a little sheepish. "As much as one can be at a murder trial."

"What can we do to help, sir?" Dawson asked.

The chief looked at his watch. "Lorraine Taylor's plane should be touching down in forty-five minutes and nobody has given me an option that I'm happy with."

Chase took a sideways glance at Dawson. There were a number of safe houses that they used in the city, even a few in West County. Those were the ones he knew about. The chief probably knew of others.

"Her location was compromised in Miami," Chief Bates said. "I can't have that happen here. She's already not happy about coming to the same city where Malone is sitting in jail. I'm thinking of stashing her downstate, maybe Springfield."

Chase could see the concern on Dawson's face. He would not want to be hours away from his wife if the baby decided to come early. He waited to see if Dawson would say something. But he didn't. Chase understood. Turning down an assignment that the chief personally handed you was career suicide.

Chase leaned forward in his chair. He was

going to regret this. "My brothers and I own a house in Ravesville. It's sitting empty right now. It's a mile and a half outside of town. Only a couple neighbors on the same road. Brick...uh, my stepfather just died."

The chief's eyes lit up. "Did you grow up there?"

Chase nodded.

"When did you move away?"

He'd left the day Calvin had turned eighteen, when both of them were legal to be on their own. He'd been twenty-one. "Thirteen years ago, sir. I went back once, about eight years ago."

The chief tapped his middle finger on the wood desk. He stared at it. Finally, he looked up. "I like it. We'll have your file reflect that you're on personal leave. If anybody asks," he said, looking at Dawson, "Detective Hollister is dealing with family stuff. Nobody besides the two of you and the few people that I personally involve will have any knowledge of the truth. Nobody else."

He switched his laser-sharp gaze to Chase. "Congratulations, Detective Hollister. You just got married. Lorraine Taylor can pose as your wife."

Chapter Two

By the time the plane had landed and Luis was hustling her through the airport, Raney had a headache that wouldn't quit. They exited into a wall of very warm, humid air.

"I thought the Midwest was cooler than Florida," she said.

Luis didn't respond. He was busy looking at his phone. Then he signaled for a cab.

"Where are we going?" she asked.

"I don't know," he said, sounding irritated. "I just got a text with a street address from my contact."

"That makes me feel very secure," she said drily. Sweat was gathering between her breasts and the hot sun made her feel sick to her stomach. "You'd think they'd at least spring for a car," she said grumpily.

Again Luis did not respond, which surprised her. In Florida he'd been polite, almost chatty.

He'd been quiet on the plane. Now he seemed edgy. It made her feel off balance.

The cab drove for about thirty minutes before finally pulling into an empty spot behind a brown UPS truck. The driver was out of the vehicle, stacking boxes high on a cart.

It dawned on her that she was just another kind of package. She'd been wrapped up and sent halfway across the country, to be handed off into someone else's care. And they were going to cart her somewhere else and put her on a shelf for a month.

She looked at the sign in the nearest store window. It was a frozen yogurt shop. At least things were looking up. "Is this it?"

Luis didn't answer. He was watching the street closely. They got out of the cab and hadn't walked more than three feet before a big man, probably close to the age her father would have been, fell into step next to them. He had a plastic bag looped over one hand.

He nodded at her and spoke quietly to Luis. Luis extended his hand and the men shook. Luis turned to her. "This is police chief Bates. He'll take over from here."

"Great," she said.

"We're happy to have you in St. Louis," the man said. "Thank you, Officer Vincenze."

Luis nodded at the chief and looked at her.

"Good luck," he said before turning quickly away. He got back into the same cab they'd arrived in. Chief Bates waited until the cab had pulled away from the curb before turning toward her.

"Rest assured that we're going to keep you perfectly safe," he said. "Right now we need to get a few things taken care of."

"What things?" she asked.

"I'll answer all your questions," he said. They walked past the frozen yogurt shop. Turned a corner. Walked another block. Turned another corner. Second store in, he stopped. "But first, let's just step inside here." He opened the door to what appeared to be a hair salon. The lights inside were dimmed and there were no customers. Just a woman standing behind the high counter.

"Morning, Marvin," the woman said.

"Ms. Taylor, this is my sister, Sandy. Work your magic, honey," the chief said to the woman.

The day was getting stranger by the minute.

An hour later, Raney's shoulder-length brown hair had been chopped off and she was a platinum blonde. Without the heavy weight, her hair had a natural wave that surprised her. She liked that she could tuck the wispy strands behind her ears. She also had to admit that the new hair color made her light blue eyes pop in a way that eye shadow had never managed. It was a startling change and she had trouble taking it all in.

"She's done," Sandy said. They were the first words she'd spoken since she explained that she was going to lighten up and trim her hair. Sandy was clearly a master of understatement.

The chief, who had looked ridiculous perched on one of the small chairs in the waiting area, stood up. "Everybody else should be here soon."

He was right if "everybody" was three men. She could see them through the glass window. One was in his midfifties with a camera around his neck, carrying what appeared to be a big bag of dry cleaning. The second was a handsome black man dressed in a nice gray suit. The third man, and the one who held her attention, was in a tux and carried a small suitcase with him. He was tall.

If Sandy planned to trim him up, she didn't have much to work with. His dark brown hair was already cut short, maybe not military short but pretty close. It showed off his chiseled good looks.

The chief opened the door and locked it behind them. The room was suddenly filled with testosterone. Raney, who was still sitting in the stylist's chair, felt at a disadvantage. She stood up quickly, tried to take a step, got the heel of her sandal caught in the lower rung of the chair and pitched forward.

Tuxedo Guy caught her before she landed on her face. His grip on her bare upper arms was secure but light. He gently pushed her upright and she passed within inches of his body.

He smelled delicious, an earthy citrus that evoked images of a tropical rainforest.

"Okay?" he asked, his voice low, sexy. His skin was very tan and his eyes were an odd shade of brown, almost amber.

"Ah, sure," she managed. She'd been off balance since leaving Florida and the past fifteen seconds hadn't helped. Who was this man?

"Ms. Taylor," Chief Bates said. "You need to get changed."

Huh?

The man with the camera extended his dry cleaning in her direction. She automatically reached out, noting the bag was heavier than it looked.

Sandy pointed to a door. Raney stood her ground. "Maybe you're thinking that someone has explained to me what's going on, but nobody has. And I don't think I'm changing my clothes or anything else until somebody does."

The black man looked at Chief Bates. Tuxedo Guy was staring at her, and she thought she caught a glimpse of appreciation in his eyes.

"Of course," the chief said. "I apologize. I'm just anxious to get you to a safe place. This is Officer Henderson. He's a photographer for the police department. This is Detective Roy and Detective Hollister."

"Thank you," she said. "Why do I need new clothes? I have my own," she said, inclining her head toward her suitcase, which was still sitting near the front door.

"There's a wedding dress in there," the chief said. "You need to put it on and Officer Henderson is going to snap a few pictures of you and Detective Hollister as the happy bride and groom. He's assured me that he's managed to manipulate the date on his camera so if anyone digs into the pictures, they'll believe they were taken several weeks ago, on August 15. We've filed a license with the county clerk's office dated that same day in case someone bothers to check. Under a different name, of course."

She felt her face grow hot. What was this guy smoking? Wedding dress? Marriage license? Different name? "I'm not getting married," she said. She'd been married. It hadn't gone well.

Chief Bates looked as if he wasn't used to people disagreeing with his plans. Detective Roy stepped forward. "Of course not," he said. "Your cover for the next month while we await Harry Malone's trial will be as Detective Hollister's wife. You'll be living at Chase's parents' home in rural Missouri, about two hours from here."

Her head, maybe feeling light because she'd lost a lot of hair or maybe because she was in an alternate universe, swiveled on her neck. She stared at Tuxedo Guy. "We're going to be married," she repeated. "Actually, we're already married, if the wedding was August 15," she said, rather stupidly she thought, the minute the words were out of her mouth.

"I guess that's right," he said.

"And we're going to live with your parents?"

He shook his head. "They're dead. The house is empty."

She rubbed her forehead. "What's my new name?" she asked.

Chief Bates stepped forward. "In these types of situations, it's better if we can keep your first name the same. Less confusion for you. In the event of an emergency, you'll react to it better. We'll list your maiden name on the wedding certificate as Lorraine Smith. It's common enough. Then, of course, you'll be Lorraine Hollister for the duration of this assignment."

"Somewhere in Missouri," she said.

"Yes, ma'am," Chief Bates said.

She clutched her wedding dress tighter. "I swear to God, if I ever get a chance at Harry Malone, I'm going to kill him myself."

THE BLOND HAIR had set him back because it was such a dramatic difference from the picture he'd studied on the way over to the hair salon. In the photo, her brown hair had hung past her shoulders, her face had been pale and her eyes had been dark with fatigue. It had likely been taken the morning that she'd first been interviewed by the Miami police after her ordeal with Harry Malone had ended.

Today, she looked amazing. The hair was sexy, her skin was clear and fresh and her blue eyes were gorgeous. She would make a pretty bride.

Once Chief Bates had determined the plan, they'd swung into action. The chief had left to intercept Lorraine Taylor. Chase had been dispatched home to pack a suitcase and then to the mall to get a tux. He had met Dawson back at the police station and they'd picked up Gavin Henderson, who'd been busy in his own right. He'd been sent home to get his daughter's recently cleaned wedding dress. All of them, including the chief, had been at her wedding five weeks earlier.

Dawson had managed to pull him aside before they'd piled into the car. "I know why you offered up the house in Ravesville," he'd said. "And I appreciate it."

"It's no problem," Chase had replied, lying. He hated the idea.

"Newlyweds?" Dawson had needled. "You going to be okay with that?"

Dawson was well aware that Chase wasn't interested in marriage. Even so, because he was besotted with his own bride, Dawson had a tendency to overencourage Chase to commit and ragged his tail when Chase easily dismissed the idea. It had gotten to the point that Chase had stopped telling him about his occasional dates because the man made too damn big a deal out of them.

That, of course, had led Dawson to worry that Chase was becoming a monk. "You're not getting any younger," he said. "You might want to catch one while you're still in your prime."

He sure as hell wasn't going to admit to Dawson that his leg now ached as though he was ninety.

The next month was going to suck but he'd make the best of it. He was pretty confident

Lorraine Taylor felt the same way. When she'd said *Missouri*, it had sounded an awful lot like *misery*. She hadn't slammed the door when she'd gone to change into the wedding dress but she'd surely looked as if she wanted to.

But as much as he hated the idea, he had to admit, it wasn't a terrible plan. No one would question his presence at the house. After all, he and his brothers had lived there for many years and it would be common knowledge in the small community that Brick had recently died. People there would be expecting somebody from the family to come back and take care of the property.

Now, courtesy of some just-in-time photography, Dawson was going to upload the wedding photos onto a couple social media sites, publicizing that he'd recently done best-man honors for Chase and his happy bride. That way if anyone bothered to search for Chase Hollister, the cover story would hold. Chief Bates had instructed that if anyone at the department happened across the photos and asked, Dawson was to hold tight to the cover story. Once the trial was over, Chase could tell people the truth.

It had the potential to be a win-win. He'd be there to watch over Lorraine. He'd also be able to get the house ready for sale, and the State of Missouri would preserve their witness in what was likely to be one of the biggest trials of the year.

He and Lorraine simply needed to act the part of happy newlyweds. He heard the door open and in a rustle of silk and lace, Lorraine stepped out into the hallway, wearing the wedding dress. She was blushing.

"I'm going to need some help with the zipper," she said.

None of the men moved. Chase was pretty sure he'd stopped breathing.

Finally, Sandy got behind her and Chase heard the gentle rasp of a zipper. With every inch, Chase felt his mouth get drier. She was beautiful. Once the zipper was up, the dress hugged her curves and the cut showed a generous portion of her pretty breasts that, quite frankly, hadn't been all that visible in the T-shirt that she had been wearing.

Dawson looked at him, his dark eyes wide with speculation. Chase ignored him.

"Let's get this over with," Chief Bates instructed. He bent down, opened the plastic sack at his feet and proved that he hadn't wasted time while waiting for Lorraine's plane to land. He pulled out two items. The first one was flowers. They were wrapped in clear plastic and Chase recognized them as the kind you could buy for fifteen bucks at the grocery store. The chief thrust them toward Lorraine.

She didn't move, just stared at them.

"Hang on," Sandy said. She opened a drawer, pulled out a pair of scissors and efficiently cut off the plastic wrap, then trimmed off the long stems. When she finished, it was a very presentable bouquet.

The second item in Chief Bates's bag was a birthday cake. With pink and yellow balloons on it. "This was all they had," he apologized.

Chase thought he caught the glimpse of a smile on Lorraine's face.

"I can make it work," Gavin said. "Chase and Lorraine, I need you to stand in front of this wall."

Chase moved to where Gavin pointed. After a second of hesitation, Lorraine did the same. Up close, he realized that he was probably about eight inches taller than her, which gave him a truly excellent view down the front of her dress.

He felt his whole body get warm.

He jerked his head up and stared at Gavin, who had his camera out. The man looked up, irritation on his face. "I can add a church background with Photoshop but I can't make the two of you look happy. Come on. Work with me."

Chase licked his lips and sucked in a deep

breath. Then he wrapped his arm around Lorraine's shoulders. He bent his head, looked into her eyes and gave her his best smile.

He thought she might tell him to go to hell. But after a long minute of staring into his eyes, she pasted on her own smile.

And for the next fifteen minutes, he and Lorraine Taylor responded like trained seals. Gavin snapped pictures of them facing one another, side by side and even feeding each other pieces of cake off plastic plates that Sandy had found in the bottom drawer of her desk. Snap, snap, snap. Finally, Gavin instructed him to move out of the frame and for Lorraine to give the camera her back. "Pretend you're just about to throw your bouquet," he said.

She did. Snap, snap, snap. Then he said, "Okay. I've got enough."

Lorraine let the flowers sail. Without thinking, Chase reached out to catch them. When she turned, her blue eyes were big.

"Congratulations, Detective," she said. "I guess a real wedding is in your future."

Chase let the flowers fall to the ground. Everyone in the room stared at them.

Gavin coughed loudly. "Let's finish up with the groom kissing the bride."

Chase felt his racing heart skip a beat. He

looked at Lorraine. He no longer felt like a trained seal but rather a fish out of water.

"Ready?" he said.

"Ready," she whispered.

He walked close and bent his head, intending to merely brush her lips.

"Make it look good," Gavin said.

She opened her mouth and he felt himself settle in. She tasted like chocolate cake and her mouth was warm and wet, and it had been a long time since a kiss had made his knees weak.

But when it was over, he had to admit that this one had done just that.

But he sure as hell wasn't going to give Dawson the satisfaction of seeing it. "Is that a wrap?" he asked, making sure that his tone was nonchalant.

He ignored the soft hiss he heard from Lorraine.

"We need to hit the road," he said. "I want to get to Ravesville before dark."

DETECTIVE HOLLISTER WAS an amazing kisser. His lips had been warm, his breath sweet and his hands confident as they'd cupped her face. It was as if someone had hit a switch, kicking off an electrical charge that had started in her toes and rapidly spread through her body.

She'd felt alive.

And she'd been stupid enough to think that it had affected him the same way. Of course it hadn't. And she suspected she should be grateful that he'd been an ass about it afterward because she had been about thirty seconds away from crawling up his body.

That would have been a real photo opportunity.

There weren't going to be any more kisses. Not that Chase was probably inclined. He might have played the role of besotted groom, but she could tell that he hadn't been thrilled to be participating in the farcical marriage. After their ceremony, he had quickly changed into jeans and a T-shirt and, if possible, had looked even hotter. But his attitude didn't match.

He was polite. Definitely. But she'd sensed his irritation when they'd had to kill thirty minutes at the salon. She'd looked through the tattered magazines spread about the various tables and he'd focused on his smart phone.

Chief Bates had been insistent that they wait while the photographer ran a quick errand. He'd come back with a driver's license for Lorraine Hollister that in every way looked real. She suspected they probably had a back room at the police station where credentials were fabricated on a routine basis.

She'd looked at her picture. Who was this woman? This blonde Raney. She'd tossed it into her purse and they'd left without further delay.

Chase had continued to be polite. Had carried her suitcase and opened the car door for her. Waited until she was buckled in before he took off. "Cool enough?" he'd asked ten minutes into the journey, nodding at the air-conditioning controls.

Other than that, he hadn't said a word.

Which maybe worked okay for him, but it wasn't helping her acclimate to her new life.

"I can't imagine that you're any happier about this than I am," she said finally.

He shrugged, never taking his eyes off the road. "It's important to keep you safe. I can do that," he added confidently.

"What's the plan once we get to Ravesville? Should I be mentally preparing myself for a big wedding reception?" she asked, trying for humor.

He turned to look at her. "Have you ever lived in a small town?"

She shook her head. "I'm a city girl."

He looked back at the road. "Here's how it works in small towns. On our way to the house, we'll stop for dinner at the local café. Not sure of the name of it any longer but for as long as I was in Ravesville, there was always a café on the corner of Main Street and Highway 20. I'm sure it's still there. I'll casually mention my name and that I'm back in town to take care of the old house and that I've brought along my new wife. By the time we get to dessert, the story will have reached half the community and by morning, the other half will have heard."

"Fascinating," she said.

"Not really, just the way it is. After that, Lorraine, I hope that you'll spend most of your time at the house, where it will be easier to provide protection."

"Raney," she said. "I go by Raney. Not Lorraine."

He seemed to consider that. "What did Harry Malone know you as?"

"He called me Lorraine. That was what was on my name tag. And because he was only at Next Steps a couple times before…well, before, he probably didn't hear anybody refer to me differently."

There was a significant pause and she could hear the tires on the rough highway. Finally, he turned to her and said, "Raney it is."

She was relieved that he hadn't pushed for more details. Even though she'd told the story several times, it still made her sick to talk about her time with Harry Malone. Pushing that image aside, she closed her eyes and focused on the way her name had sounded on his lips. *Raney.*

As if he knew her. Which of course he didn't. No more than she knew him. This was simply his job.

And given that somebody had tried twice to kill her, she sure as hell hoped he was good at it. He'd sounded confident when he'd said he could keep her safe. "So how long have you been on the job?" she asked.

He glanced her way, surprise in his eyes. "You know a lot of cops?"

She shrugged. "A few. Why?"

"Because when most people ask that question, they ask, 'How long have you been a police officer?' It's a subtle difference but one that a cop notices."

She waited. She wasn't ready yet to tell him about her work at Next Steps, about some of the people whom she'd helped, some of the people who had needed a hand. She'd virtually stooped, cupped her hands and given them a foothold. She was proud of her work, knew the impact she'd had.

"I've been a cop for thirteen years," he said. "Covered a beat for eight of those before I became a detective. I mostly work homicides."

"But you've done witness protection work before?" she asked.

"I have. I know what I'm doing," he said. She could tell that she'd offended him.

"I'm sorry," she said. "It's just that…"

"I know," he said, his tone gentler.

"So you live in St. Louis?"

"Yes."

They drove a few more miles. The silence in the SUV was oppressive. "In a house?" Lately she'd had houses on the brain.

He shook his head. "A thirty-year mortgage isn't my style," he said. "I've got a six-month lease on an apartment in the Central West End."

"What happens after six months?"

He shrugged. "I sign another lease. Or I don't."

"How long have you lived there?"

"Five years."

That was weird. He'd been on the job for thirteen years and lived in the same apartment for five years but he was still only interested in a six-month lease. Maybe that was how things were done in the Central West End.

She had no idea where that was but assumed it was likely sort of upscale, like Chase. He wore a nice watch, good leather shoes, had nice manners and he'd looked very comfortable in a tux.

"I've been saving for a house," she admitted. "I love my apartment building and my neighbors but lately, I've been thinking that it's time for me to get a house. But now… I'm not sure. Maybe the security of having neighbors close by is what I need."

He took his eyes off the road in order to look at her again. "You've had a tough couple of months. Don't make any big decisions right now. Sit back, consider, then act when you're ready."

Others had given her the same advice, although not in those exact words. She let out the breath she'd been holding. Maybe in Ravesville, she could do that. Just relax.

She felt the ever-present knot in her stomach release just a little. Now the quiet was no longer oppressive. It felt safe. Nice. She closed her eyes and didn't open them again until she felt someone lightly shaking her shoulder.

"We're here," he said.

She was surprised to see that it was getting dark. She looked at the clock on the dash. Twenty minutes after six. Her stomach rumbled and she pressed the palm of her hand against it.

"I imagine you're hungry," he said.

She'd had toast for breakfast, nothing for lunch and a bite of cake that he'd popped into her mouth. "Yes," she said, turning her neck slowly to get the kinks out. "So this is it?"

It was a wide street, lined with freshly painted perpendicular parking spaces. The buildings were mostly old, lots of red brick, nothing over three stories. There were a few flower boxes with brightly colored mums below the windows and some more pots scattered down the sidewalk. There was an empty bike rack at the end of the block.

He'd been right about the restaurant. The Wright Here, Wright Now Café had its lights on and there were a few cars parked in front of the two-story brick building. Other than that, the only other cars were three or four gathered together at the end of the next block. "What's down there?" she asked, pointing. "Besides the edge of town?"

"A bar. Everything else closes up tight in the evenings."

She'd grown up in Manhattan and moved to Miami when she was sixteen, after her mom got a new job as the general counsel for an insurance company. Her dad had been a writer and had worked from home. They'd been killed by a drunk driver four years later. She'd stayed in Florida, hadn't really had anyplace else to go. While not Manhattan, Miami was still a large city where they didn't roll up the streets at half past six.

"I hope the food is good," she said, almost under her breath.

"Don't get your hopes up," he said. "But we need to eat. I'm not confident that there will be anything at the house."

They got out of the car. When Chase crossed in front of the hood, she thought she saw just a hint of a limp. She hadn't noticed it before. "Did you hurt your leg?" she asked.

He waved it off. "Stiff from driving," he said.

"So how did your stepfather die?" she asked as they walked down the sidewalk toward the restaurant.

"Car accident."

"I'm sorry," she said. "Was it a big funeral?"

He didn't answer. But he did hold the door open for her. She walked into the restaurant. It was brightly lit. There were three tables with customers. On the nine other available tables, there were tan paper placemats and silverware wrapped in white paper napkins.

A woman, maybe midthirties, with gorgeous long red hair to her waist pulled back into a low ponytail, walked through the swinging door at the rear of the restaurant. She carried plates in both hands. She gave them a quick smile, but when her gaze settled on Chase, it faded.

She set her plates down with a thud, startling the older couple at the table, who also turned to stare at the two of them.

"Damn you, Chase Hollister," she said. "You just cost me ten bucks. I bet that you wouldn't come back."

Chapter Three

She watched as Chase reached into his pocket, pulled out a ten-dollar bill and handed it to the woman. "Now we're even."

The woman threw her head back and laughed. "How's your good-for-nothing brother?" she asked.

"Still thinks he's the boss of me," Chase said.

She laughed again. "Nobody was ever the boss of you, that's for sure. People round here still talk about some of the stuff you pulled."

Hmm... Was it possible that there was more to Detective Hollister than his professional attitude let on?

Chase turned toward her. "This is my wife, Raney," he said smoothly, as if it were really true and he'd been introducing her for a long time as his wife. "Raney, this is Trish Wright."

"Wright-Roper," the woman corrected.

"Didn't realize you were married," Chase said.

"Widowed," she said.

"I'm sorry," Chase apologized, sounding as if he meant it.

The pretty woman shrugged but Raney could tell that the pain was still there. But she lifted her chin and extended a hand in Raney's direction.

There was a history between Chase and Trish but Raney couldn't quite put her finger on it. Not lovers. But something. She shook the woman's hand.

"Been to the old place yet?" Trish asked.

"Nope. Just got into town."

"You'll have your work cut out for you," she said. "It's gone downhill in the past few years."

Chase shrugged as if the news didn't bother him. But Raney saw him swallow hard. "Not planning on staying there long," he said.

"Well, don't be a stranger while you're here," she said. "I know Summer would like to see you. She works the day shift." Trish grabbed two menus from the counter and led them to a table in the corner of the café. Raney noticed that Chase didn't make eye contact with any-one else in the room.

They sat down. "Old friend?" Raney mur-mured, opening her menu.

He nodded. "I've known Trish since I was a kid. My older brother, Bray, dated Summer,

Trish's sister. I always thought they might get married someday but he enlisted in the marines right out of high school and she married some other guy."

"How long since you've been in Ravesville?"

"I came back once, about eight years ago, when my mother died. Other than that, thirteen years," he said. "What are you having for dinner?" he asked, quickly changing the subject.

So he hadn't come for his stepfather's funeral. That was why he hadn't known whether it was big or small. But he clearly didn't want to talk about it. She tried to tell herself that she didn't care. She didn't need his life story. She just needed a place to stay where she'd be safe. Someplace in the middle of Missouri was as good as any.

When Trish returned, pen in hand, Raney closed her menu. "I'll take a salad with grilled…" She caught a glimpse of her reflection and almost jerked back in surprise. The change was almost too much to take in. If Sandy had been more forthcoming about the intended results, she'd have probably bolted from the chair.

But she was glad that she hadn't. She liked the new look. Had never considered going blond but now she might never go back.

One thing she could thank Harry Malone for.

"Actually," she said. "No salad. I'll take a bacon cheeseburger. With fries."

Chase ordered the meat loaf. Once Trish had walked away, he looked at her. "Salad just wasn't going to cut it?" he asked, obviously trying to think of something to say.

She was going to shrug it off but then decided that if they were going to live together for the next month as husband and wife, she needed to be honest with him. "That would have been BHM. Before Harry Malone. Now I pretty much treat myself to whatever I want, when I want it."

Come to think of it, maybe that was why she was digging the new haircut and look. It *fit* the new Raney Taylor. The Raney Taylor that she was molding.

He studied her, then spoke quietly but with conviction. "If it's any consolidation, the son of a bitch is going to pay. He's going to go to prison and, trust me on this, there will be somebody there that will make his life a living hell."

She was counting on that.

When Trish delivered their food, it looked delicious. She picked up her burger, squished the bun so that it would fit in her mouth and took a bite. A bit of sauce leaked out and she licked her lips. And then swallowed too quickly when she realized that he was watching her.

"Ouch," she said, pressing on her esophagus.

"Careful," he said.

She always used to be. And look where it had gotten her. "So what did you do to earn your reputation as the town bad boy?" she asked.

He scratched his head. "A little of this, a lot of that."

"And you became a cop to redeem yourself?"

"I became a cop because the St. Louis Police Department was hiring and I needed a way to support myself and my younger brother. Fortunately for me, it was a good fit. Maybe because of my troublemaking youth."

She took another bite, smaller this time. "There wasn't much you hadn't seen or done."

He smiled and shook his head. "Trust me on this. I might have made some people talk here in Ravesville but what I was doing was kid's play in comparison to what I saw my first six months on the street."

"So you were just naughty enough to cause your parents some angst."

His very nice amber eyes clouded over. "Something like that."

They ate in silence. Trish swung by and

picked up their dirty plates and left a check. Chase pulled some bills out of his pocket and tossed them on the table.

"Ready?" he asked.

WHEN HIS WIFE nodded that she was good to go, he almost said, *Hell no, let's have some cheesecake.* Anything to delay a trip back down memory lane.

But he wasn't going to make it any better by putting it off. He led her back to the car and drove a mile and half farther on the highway before taking a right on Mahogany Lane. The road turned to gravel and he slowed his SUV. He passed the Fitzlers' house and noticed that there were lights on. Was it possible that Old Man Fitzler and his wife still lived there? Or maybe they'd moved on to one of those assisted-living centers and one of their daughters had moved in.

Damn, he'd envied those girls.

He didn't think Mr. Fitzler had ever even raised his voice, let alone his hand.

He slowed the vehicle even more and turned into the driveway. His lights picked up the details of the old house.

Over a hundred years old, the two-story white farmhouse looked sturdy enough. It had been the traditional four rooms down, kitchen, dining room, living room and bath, and four rooms up, three bedrooms and a bath, until sometime in the mid-1960s. The owner had pushed out the back wall and added to the downstairs, putting in another large bedroom and private bathroom. They'd done a nice job with the construction and the addition seemed to fit nicely with the rest of the house.

When Chase's parents had looked at the home some ten years later, it had seemed perfect to the young couple who were anxious to have a family. Chase always figured that once three boys had come along, his mother had been eternally grateful that she could ship them upstairs.

There were a few changes, Chase noted dispassionately. Brick had added green shutters at some point in the past eight years. They hadn't been there when Chase and his brothers had come home for his mother's funeral.

The wide wraparound porch looked the same, down to the hammock that was strung in the corner. He'd slept in that more than a few times. Nights when it was warm and he chose to. Nights when it was cold and Brick had banished him from the house. Those were the nights when he'd wanted to keep walking, to wake up somewhere else, but he would not do that to his mother, to Cal.

The bushes near the foundation were wildly overgrown and as he pulled closer, he could see that the paint on the house was peeling and the front steps looked as if they were rotting away in places.

He chanced a glance at Raney. Her eyes were moving, taking it in.

She was probably getting ready to bolt from the car. "Hopefully, it's better inside."

She shrugged. "It's got good bones," she said. "I love the porch and all the big windows."

Brick had pushed Calvin's hand through one of those windows one winter night. That was when Chase and the man had come to a deal of sorts.

He turned off the car and killed the lights. It made him realize how dark the yard was. "Watch your step," he said when she opened her door.

They each grabbed their own suitcase and picked their way across the patchy grass. When they reached the long sidewalk that led to the house, he stopped. Bray had sent him a text letting him know that the attorney was putting a key in the mailbox. Chase flipped down the rusted aluminum door and sure enough, it was there.

He led the way up the sidewalk and stairs

and onto the porch. "Be careful," he warned again. He unlocked the door, pushed it open, listened for a minute but didn't hear anything. He reached his hand around to feel for the light switch and, he had to admit, felt better when light flooded the area.

To the right was the living room with a couch and two chairs that he didn't recognize and to the left, the dining room with his mother's big wooden table. He glanced down the hallway. In the back of the house, still in darkness, would be the big kitchen. It had a window over the sink and his mother had loved to stand there and watch the deer and the wild turkeys wander through the backyard.

At some point Brick had painted the dark brown woodwork white, but it must have been a poor grade of paint because it was peeling in multiple places. There were cracks in the plaster walls and multiple brown patches on the ceiling, suggesting that rain had leaked into the second floor all the way to the first floor. That wasn't a good sign.

He flipped on additional lights as they walked. When they entered the kitchen, the first thing he saw was the open newspaper on the table, along with a half-drank cup of tea with the bag still in it. Out of habit, he felt the cup. It was stone cold.

There was a dirty plate in the sink. Brick had had eggs for his last meal.

He opened the refrigerator. Not full by any means, but there were small packages of cheese and lunchmeat, some half-used bottles of salad dressing and ketchup, and a quart of milk. Something, he wasn't sure what, had spilled at some point on the top shelf and dripped down, leaving remains all the way to the bottom. It smelled sweet.

Brick had gotten sloppy in his old age. Or maybe he'd always been a pig and Sally Hollister had managed to cover up for him.

He turned, realizing that Raney had ventured off into the direction of the downstairs bedroom. He followed her, his chest feeling tighter with each step. He didn't want to look at Brick's bedroom, didn't want to have that intimate of a connection to the man.

Raney stopped in the doorway. Chase stood behind her. There was a regular-size bed, made up with an ugly shiny green bedspread. The matching drapes were drawn tight, giving the room an eerie feel. The gold paint on the walls made the room look dirty. The door to the bathroom was open. With its dated green fixtures, it looked exactly like he remembered.

He sure as hell wasn't sleeping down here. "Let's take a look upstairs," he said.

The wooden steps creaked as they made their way upstairs. He saw Raney flick her hand over her hair and realized she'd disturbed a large cobweb. The carpet in the hallway was threadbare and all the doors were closed.

"I don't think your stepfather was up here much," Raney said.

He nodded and opened the first door. This had been Bray's room. He felt for the light switch and flipped it up. The room was completely empty.

He walked down the hall a few steps toward his old room. He turned the handle of the door, expecting it to open, but it didn't.

The door was locked. And for some crazy reason, that irritated the hell out of him. Without conscious thought, Chase lifted his good leg and kicked the damn door. It flew back, breaking the top hinge. He heard Raney's gasp but he ignored it. He felt for the light switch, flipped it and, when nothing happened, he stepped back so that light from the hallway could filter in.

The room was completely empty. He looked up at the ceiling light fixture. Even the lightbulb had been removed.

"Do you think perhaps there's an air mattress somewhere?" Raney asked, her tone light.

There was only one bedroom left to try.

Cal's. The door swung open and the light worked. In the middle of the room was a queen-size mattress, still with its plastic wrapper, without any bedding or even a bed frame. The mattress and box spring sat directly on the wood floor. There was a bedside table with a lamp. There was no other furniture in the room.

Why the hell had Brick bought a new mattress and put it upstairs in Cal's old room? And never put sheets or a blanket on it? Based on the layer of dust on the plastic, the mattress had been up here for some time. It wasn't as if Brick had done it recently and just hadn't finished the project.

Well, whatever the reason, it wasn't great but it was better than sleeping on the wood floor. "You can sleep in here," he said. He pulled a pocketknife out of his jeans, sliced open the plastic and ripped it off the mattress. Dust flew into the air and she sneezed.

"Sorry," he said. "We can get some sheets tomorrow."

She sat down on the edge of the mattress. "Where will you sleep?" she asked.

"Downstairs. On the couch. There's no reason to believe that anybody knows that Lorraine Taylor is in this house. But if anything scares you, just yell. I'm a light sleeper. I'll hear you."

She looked around the room. She sighed a little dramatically. "All these years and I never ever envisioned my wedding night would go exactly like this."

For the first time since Chief Bates had announced that he and Lorraine Taylor were posing as husband and wife, he felt like smiling. She was being a good sport. Her last safe house had no doubt been better.

He wanted to promise that everything would look better in the light of day but based on what he'd seen tonight, he thought the opposite was probably true. He would not have volunteered to bring her to Ravesville if he'd known the house was in this bad of shape.

"Good night," he said.

He stuck his head into the bathroom that was across the hall. Ran the water in the faucet until it turned clear and flushed the toilet a couple times. There was toilet paper but it was covered with a layer of dust. He unrolled several sheets, ripped them off, and threw them in the small empty garbage can. There were no towels so he ran downstairs, got several clean ones from the cupboard in the downstairs bathroom and took them back upstairs.

It wasn't camping but it was close.

Finally, he went back downstairs and, still fully dressed, stretched out on the couch. It was too short for him and his feet hung over the edge. He was so damn tired. He hadn't been kidding when he'd told his brother that he'd been awake for more than a day. He had managed to grab some sleep after he'd talked to Dawson but the knowledge that the chief was counting on them had weighed heavily on his mind.

Now, even though his body craved rest, he lay awake, staring at the ceiling, his mind trying to wrap itself around the fact that he was back in Ravesville, back in the house that he'd left thirteen years ago, swearing that he'd never return.

On the drive here, he'd wondered if he'd feel Brick in the house. Or even his mother. But the house just felt empty, so empty it seemed as if there had never been life here.

But that wasn't true. There had been life and love when Jack Hollister had been alive. His father would have despised Brick, would have hated what had become of the family.

As odd as it seemed, he could feel his father in the house. He hadn't been able to do that when Brick was alive and living here. But now it felt very different. It was almost as if he could see him standing in front of the big windows, waving at him and his brothers to come in for dinner. Could see him walking through the house, a fishing pole in one hand and sack lunches in the other, yelling for his sons to hurry up, that the trout were biting.

As if he'd conjured up old spirits, he heard a noise. Something soft. Outside. He eased off the couch, used a finger to pull back the heavy drapes and watched the yard.

Nothing moved in the darkness. He waited, continuing to watch. Five minutes later, a dark shape, low to the ground, crossed the gravel.

A groundhog. He let out the breath he'd been holding. He'd been spooked by an animal.

He lay back down, rubbed his sore thigh and closed his eyes. Upstairs, he heard a door open and close, then the sound of water running through the pipes as Raney turned on the shower. She'd had a hell of a day but had seemed to handle it well. She'd been shot at yesterday, hustled out of Florida this morning, pushed into a fake marriage and had ended up here, in a house of neglect.

He'd clean up the place tomorrow, at least get the top layer of dust off. Then he would pitch everything in the refrigerator and make a quick trip to town for food. If the dinner Raney had eaten tonight was any indication, she had a good appetite. Which was surprising considering she was pretty slim.

But the curves were there. He'd seen that firsthand in the wedding dress. That image had stayed with him the entire drive from St. Louis to Ravesville. That and the memory of the feel of her mouth.

He heard the water shut off. Let himself have the guilty pleasure of imaging Raney's wet body stepping over the edge of the old tub. Of her drying off on the threadbare towel.

He heard the door open and the floor creak as she crossed the hall. He wondered if she'd brought pajamas or if she slept naked.

He let out a breath, happy to let that image rest on his brain.

WHEN HE WOKE UP, the sun was low in the sky. He checked the time. A little past seven. He sat up, stretched and went in search of coffee.

There was no coffeepot on the counter. He opened cupboards. Not even a jar of instant. It was another reason to despise Brick.

He walked up the stairs and muscle memory kicked in, making it easy for him to avoid the same squeaky boards that had been there thirteen years ago. Raney's bedroom door was closed. He considered knocking but decided against it.

She probably needed her sleep.

He opened the door and stopped. The woman knew how to take up a bed. She slept on her stomach with her head at ten o'clock and her feet at four o'clock. She wasn't naked but her sweet little body was plenty sexy in her lime green shorts and white-and-green-striped T-shirt. She was breathing deeply.

She'd tossed the clothes that she'd been wearing the night before into a pile. On top was her bra and panties, a silky pale yellow with lots of lace.

His face felt warm and when she stirred, he thought maybe he'd moaned.

Dawson was right. He needed to get more regular sex.

He took a step back, carefully closing the door. He could run into town, pick up some coffees and pastries from the bakery and be back before she ever woke up. Maybe that would make up for stashing her in this dump.

He left the house, making sure that he locked the door behind him. The drive to town took just minutes and when he walked into the bakery, the first thing he saw was the cakes in the display case.

It made him remember how the birthday/wedding cake had amused Raney. He debated buying another one just to see her reaction but instead got six doughnuts and a coffee cake along with two extralarge coffees.

He sipped his coffee on the way home. When he pulled into the yard, he did not notice anything amiss. Which was why, when he opened the door and looked down the hallway into the kitchen, he got caught short.

He saw the man. Catalogued his dirty blue jeans and dark sweatshirt and the greasy hair that hung to his shoulders.

Saw all that but what Chase focused on was the knife that the man held. It had a shiny six-inch blade and was raised and pointed.

At Raney.

Still in her pajamas, she had her back pressed up against the sink. Her face was pale and her eyes were big.

The man leaped toward her. Chase pulled his gun but knew that he was going to be too late.

Chapter Four

Raney twisted, brought a knee up, connected with something and used every bit of strength in her arms to push the man backward.

It was enough to buy a few seconds and give Chase a chance to leap across the space that separated them. She saw the knife go flying and within moments, Chase had the man on the ground, his knee in his chest and his gun pointed at his head.

He turned to look at her. "Are you hurt?" he asked. His eyes were dark, flashing with anger.

She managed to shake her head.

Chase looked down at the man. "Who the hell are you?" he asked, his voice hard.

The man squinted his eyes. "Get off me," he said. "You're heavy."

Raney took a closer look at the man. He'd surprised the heck out of her. She'd just gotten a drink of water when she'd heard a noise behind her. She'd turned, seen the man and the still-open back door, and realized that she was in a world of trouble.

Chase had walked in just in the nick of time.

Chase used the palm of one hand to knock the man's head back against the dirty kitchen linoleum. "Start talking."

"You need to get out of here," the man said. "You need to get out of my house right now."

Raney saw the change in Chase's eyes and realized that he'd figured something out. Good, because she didn't have a clue what was going on.

Chase let up on some of the pressure on the man's chest but he didn't let him get up. "Lloyd?" he asked.

"How do you know my name?" the man asked.

"I'm Chase. Chase Hollister."

"I know you," the man said. He smiled.

Chase looked up at Raney. "This is Lloyd Doogan. He's my stepfather's biological son."

"So you're sort of related?"

"I don't generally think of it that way." He looked back down at the man. "Lloyd, I'm going to let you get up. I'm not giving you back your knife. You need to sit, so that we can have a conversation."

Chase was speaking deliberately and didn't move until the man nodded his understanding.

Lloyd got up and sat. He looked at Raney. "Who are you?"

"Her name is Raney," Chase said, jumping in. "My wife."

Lloyd seemed to consider this. "I thought you were one of those teenagers from town. The ones who are always causing trouble."

Teenager. Granted, she wasn't dressed for success in her shorts and tank top, but she surely didn't look sixteen. Chase turned his head but not before she caught a glimpse of a smile.

"Hey!" she challenged.

"I think it's a compliment," he said, somewhat sheepishly. He turned back to Lloyd. "This house never belonged to Brick. He was just living here after my mom died. This house doesn't belong to you now. It belongs to my brothers and me."

Lloyd didn't answer. But he was frowning.

"Do you understand, Lloyd?" Chase pushed.

"He told me I could live here," Lloyd said. "A couple years ago. Said he bought me a bed and everything. But then he got mad about something, I don't even know what. All I know is that he stopped talking to me, told me I couldn't come here no more. That ain't no way to treat a son."

Chase didn't say anything.

"I hated him. I really did," Lloyd added.

"I imagine so," Chase said quietly.

Even Raney was tracking now. They might not be blood but these two men shared something.

Chase looked over his shoulder and made eye contact with her. "Lloyd," he said, his eyes still locked on her. "I need to talk to Raney. I need you to stay in your chair."

Chase pulled her to the side, keeping her back to Lloyd, which allowed him to keep his eyes on his stepbrother.

"I don't know Lloyd well," he whispered. "But I'm sure he really did think you were trespassing in his house. Now, that didn't give him a right to go at you with a knife," Chase said, his tone hard, "and if he'd managed to hurt you, we'd be having a very different conversation." He paused, looking back at Lloyd, then at her again. "We have a choice to make. We can call the police or we can pretend this never happened."

Calling the police would attract attention to them, which was what they didn't want to do. Plus, Chase would likely be putting his stepbrother in jail. By the looks of him, she thought it might be possible that the man wouldn't have the resources to post bail.

"I'm not hurt," she said. "No harm done,

right? Although we may want to make sure that we confiscate his key to the back door," she said, nodding at the silver key on the floor near Lloyd's feet. "Let him go," she added.

"You're sure?" Chase asked, his eyes searching her face.

She nodded.

"Thank you," Chase said simply.

He moved around her and sat down across from his stepbrother. "Lloyd, do you understand that I could call the police? That you would be the one in trouble because we belong here?"

Lloyd nodded.

"Do you understand that you can't come back to this house?"

Lloyd nodded again.

"I need to hear you say it," Chase prodded.

"I won't come back," Lloyd said. He shifted his gaze to Raney. "I'm sorry, ma'am, if I scared you."

Ma'am? She liked it better when he thought she was a teenager. "Raney," she corrected.

Chase picked up the key. "Lloyd, is this your only key to the house?"

"Yes. *He* never knew I had it," Lloyd said. "I sneaked into the house one day about a year ago and took it off his dresser."

She saw Chase swallow hard. "Lloyd, I'm

not going to call the police. I'm going to give you back your knife and you're going to leave the property and you're not coming back. And if you happen to see Raney again, you're going to treat her nicely, right?" Chase picked up the knife and laid it on the table, near enough for Lloyd to reach. He was watching the man closely and Raney was confident that he was still conflicted about letting him go.

"Goodbye, Lloyd," she said, hoping to give the man a hint.

Lloyd stood and picked up his knife. He kept the blade down. "Bye, ma'am." He didn't say anything to Chase. Just walked out the back door.

She and Chase went to the door. Lloyd had an old motorcycle. He got on, started it and left without giving them another look. From the back of the house, they couldn't see him after he rounded the corner but they could hear the acceleration as he turned out of the lane and headed down the highway. Then the noise faded.

The kitchen was very quiet.

"Did you know him as a boy?" she asked.

"I met him once," he said, not looking at her. "He lived with his mother. Brick didn't have anything to do with him. I'm not sure whether that was his choice or maybe his ex-wife had told him to stay away. The one time he did come around, he and Brick had a big fight. I remember my mom yelling at Brick, telling him that Lloyd didn't understand whatever Brick was trying to tell him."

"Does he live nearby?"

Chase shrugged. "I don't know." He turned, walked over to the counter, grabbed a towel from a drawer and walked back down the hallway. "I'll do some research on him, figure out where he lives and if he works. He won't surprise us again."

"I'm not worried," Raney said, following him.

Chase looked over his shoulder. "Maybe I should be. You were pretty quick with that knee. And you had good aim."

She shrugged. "You weren't so bad yourself." She looked past Chase, at the floor. "Was that coffee?" she asked, trying hard not to whine.

Chase picked up the two cups that he'd dropped. All the liquid had spilled out onto the floor. Some of it had seeped toward the bakery sack. He picked it up and opened it. "The ones on top still look fine," he said, holding out the sack.

She reached for one of the doughnuts and took a big bite. "I need coffee," she said.

"Put some different clothes on," he said. "We'll have breakfast in town."

CHASE HOPED TO hell that he'd done the right thing in letting Lloyd go. The man truly seemed to think he had a right to be in the house. And he probably had no idea that he was real lucky to still be walking and talking because Chase had been this close to wringing his neck once he'd had him subdued on the floor. All he'd been able to think about was how close the man had gotten to harming Raney.

At first, he'd given him the chance to talk because he'd wanted to know if somehow, someway, Harry Malone had managed to find them and send another goon after Raney.

Then the pieces of the puzzle had started to fit together. And when Lloyd had admitted to hating Brick, his head had started to roar. No doubt Lloyd had suffered at the man's hand, too.

He recalled his mother saying something after that one time Lloyd had been in their house, that it was a shame to be a grown man with the smarts of an eighth grader. Chase had been close to finishing high school at the time and remembered that even knowing the man had some limitations, he'd been damn jealous of him because at least he wasn't still living with Brick Doogan.

He was rubbing his injured thigh muscle when he heard Raney's footsteps on the stairs. He moved his hand quickly. His leg had taken the brunt of it when he'd tackled Lloyd and it was letting him know that it didn't appreciate it.

He looked up. She was wearing a tan-and-turquoise skirt and a sleeveless turquoise shirt. It brought out the color of her eyes. She was a beautiful woman and pretty damn brave, too. He'd known that at some level—after all, she'd managed to escape from a madman. And she'd survived another attempt on her life. But this morning, seeing her in action, seeing her willingness to fight back, had made him realize it in spades.

While she'd been upstairs, he'd sent a text to Dawson, asking him to find out everything there was to know about Lloyd Doogan. He figured he'd hear something by late afternoon.

They got in his SUV and drove the short distance into town. He took the one empty parking space that was in front of the Wright Here, Wright Now Café. Today the street was bustling with activity. People walking to their cars, into shops, chatting on the corners. There were no traffic lights, just a series of four-way-stop signs at the end of each block. It would have been a traffic nightmare in a larger city but here it was manageable.

Near the café, there was a table that hadn't been there last night. Behind it were two teenage girls in cheerleading outfits waving pompoms. The table was covered with candy bars with a big sign indicating they were two dollars a bar. He saw that Raney was staring at it. No one walked past without stopping and buying a candy bar. She opened her purse and pulled out a five-dollar bill.

"You don't have to buy anything," he said.

"Are you crazy? That's chocolate."

When they got up to the table, he saw that it was actually chocolate with caramel inside. Which must have been even better because she pulled out another one-dollar bill so that she could buy three of them. She handed one to Chase.

"In Missouri, if you're married, everything is owned fifty-fifty," he said, just low enough that she could hear.

"Oh, please. They weren't thinking about chocolate when that law passed."

Chase was smiling when he opened the door. As they walked in, he recalled what Trish had said the night before. *Summer works the day shift*. He had absolutely no difficulty identifying the woman his brother had almost married. She was at the cash register, giving change back to a customer.

"She looks so much like Trish," Raney whispered.

"She should. They're twins." They'd looked just alike in high school and there was still a great resemblance except that Summer wore her red hair shorter than Trish, just to her shoulders. He led Raney toward a booth and took the side that gave him a clear view of the door. Raney put her candy bars off to the side. He made a point of putting his in his pocket, as if he might be afraid that she'd steal it if he put it on the table.

While they were waiting to order, an older woman passed by their booth. She was carrying two candy bars. She stopped at the table and looked at Raney. "Good morning. I noticed you bought some chocolate outside."

Raney nodded.

The woman put the bars on the table. "Do take these, then. I can't eat it. But we do like to support the schools, isn't that right? You two have a good day."

"But…" Raney said.

The woman kept walking. Either she didn't hear Raney or she was ignoring her.

Chase reached for the candy bars.

Raney tapped his knuckles with her fork. "She was talking to me."

He rolled his eyes.

"Fine." She took one and pushed the other in his direction.

Summer had finished up at the cash register and was walking toward their booth. She smiled at Raney and leaned in to give Chase a hug. "Trish told me you were back," she said. "It's good to see you."

"You, too," he said. "This is my wife, Raney."

Summer extended her hand. "Welcome to Ravesville."

"Thank you," Raney said. "It smells wonderful in here."

"We bake all our own breads and muffins. Would you like to start with some coffee?"

"We'd both be eternally grateful," Chase said. He motioned to the full restaurant. "You and Trish have quite a business here."

"We love it."

Chase heard the door open and Summer must have, as well. She turned to look and her posture stiffened. Chase looked a little closer. The man was in his late thirties, balding and wore a police uniform.

"He looks familiar," Chase said quietly.

"That's Gary Blake, my ex. Excuse me," she said. "I'll be back in a minute."

"Do you know him?" Raney asked, once Summer was out of hearing distance.

Chase shook his head. "I've seen him before but it's been a long time. He was a couple years older than me."

"So he's the one that Summer married after your older brother enlisted?"

"Yeah. Guess that didn't work out so well for her," he said. "Too bad. She was always a real nice person." He picked up his menu. "What are you having?"

Raney leaned across the table. "Is your brother married?"

Chase shook his head. "Bray never married."

"Maybe you should call him. You know, tell him that you ran into Summer and she's single."

Chase closed his menu. He was glad to see the sparkle back in Raney's eyes. "Don't tell me that you're the matchmaking type."

Raney waved a hand. "I'm just saying that maybe he'd want to know."

"You're just like my partner, Dawson. He's happily married and I don't think he'll be content until the rest of the world is just like that."

"You sound like a cynic," she whispered.

"A realist. What we have is about as close to married as I plan on getting," he added.

Raney didn't say anything else because Summer returned, with two big cups of steaming coffee. The woman's cheeks were flushed. Chase had been watching her conversation with her ex. It hadn't lasted more than thirty seconds.

"Everything okay?" he asked.

"As good as ever," she said cryptically. She pulled a pad from her smock pocket. "What can I bring you?" she asked, clearly not wanting to share.

Chase ordered pancakes, eggs and bacon. Raney went for the vegetarian omelet. Summer wrote it down and stepped to the next table to take their order, too.

"What's the plan for today?" Raney asked.

"We probably need to take care of the basics," Chase said, sipping his coffee. "Get some groceries, some cleaning products, new sheets for your bed, and paint."

"We can do that in Ravesville?"

"First two can probably be had from the supermarket at the edge of town. Sheets and paint, no. We'll have to drive to Hamerton, twenty miles west. It's got a downtown that looks a lot like Ravesville but it sits close enough to the highway to have a mall and a couple big-box stores. Maybe has a couple thousand people."

Raney stared off into the distance. "When I lived in New York, there'd probably be a couple thousand people within a few blocks."

"Sounds horrific," Chase said honestly.

She shrugged. "You settled for something in the middle. St. Louis isn't New York but it's certainly not Ravesville."

He nodded. "I guess I did. It's okay for now."

"Are you thinking of leaving?" she asked, as if she expected him to bolt for the door.

He smiled. "Well, not in the middle of this assignment. But I like to keep my options open."

He'd gotten a few calls as recently as last month from headhunters who specialized in recruiting law enforcement. There had been a head of security position open for a large hotel in Chicago and his name had been recommended by someone. He'd listened to the voice mail from the recruiter but hadn't returned the call. Maybe the next one he would. Anything was possible.

She sipped her coffee. "You're lucky to have options," she said. "Many people don't. I suppose that's especially true in small towns like Ravesville."

He nodded.

She was silent for several minutes. "I guess my best hope is Ravesville is so small that whoever is behind all the crazy things that have happened doesn't know about it."

"You're safe here. I guarantee it."

At that moment, Summer delivered their food. It looked amazing and he smiled when he heard Raney's stomach growl.

Raney waited until the woman had walked away. "Well, if I have to be stranded in the sticks, I'm grateful that Summer and Trish are close by. By the way, what kind of paint are you getting?"

"Off-white."

"For?"

"Every room. Upstairs and downstairs." He could tell by the look on her face that wasn't the answer she wanted to hear. "That's what sells. Neutrals."

"But the woodwork in your house is amazing. At least it will be once that paint is stripped. And the fireplace in the living room is stunning. Off-white isn't going to work."

He rubbed his head. "What would you do?"

"Well." She leaned forward in the booth. "The dining room, a soft sage green with the windows trimmed in tan. The living room, I'd do the wall with the fireplace and the one that butts up to it in a nice brick red with the other two walls in taupe. You know, the paint colors won't actually be called this—they'll have some much fancier name—but you get the drift."

He did. She wanted to decorate and he wanted to get it cleaned up enough that a prospective buyer wouldn't run out the door.

His mother had never been much of a decorator. Perhaps she figured with three boys there was really no sense trying. And from the looks of it, Brick hadn't spent much time watching HGTV.

He didn't care enough about the house to even have this discussion. "I'm pretty set on off-white," he said.

THE GROCERY STORE wasn't big, but it had the basics. Chase went to the coffee aisle first and bought grounds and filters. "We'll get a coffeepot when we buy your sheets," he said.

Raney took control of the cart and found the produce aisle. She loaded up, selecting several of almost every fruit and vegetable they stocked while Chase, reluctantly it appeared, added a bag of chopped lettuce. When she was finally done, Chase made a point of looking at his watch. She ignored him.

She might have lost the paint discussion but she wasn't losing the grocery store. She added whole-wheat bread, cereal and skim milk. Chase added chips and peanuts. In the meat aisle, Raney picked up chicken breasts and Chase went for the ground beef. "I'm starting to see a pattern here," Raney said.

"Yeah," Chase agreed. "You're too healthy. I had high hopes for you when you ordered the bacon cheeseburger last night, and then again when I discovered you were a candy hoarder. But I can see that I was wrong."

"I'm not a hoarder, I'm a connoisseur."

In the condiment aisle, she got some olive oil and Chase grabbed mustard, mayonnaise and ketchup. "I'm throwing away everything in the refrigerator and cupboards," he said.

She couldn't argue with that. The kitchen was a hazard. She'd been trying to figure out what to do first when Lloyd had burst through the back door.

"Ready?" he asked, once they added bleach, ammonia and other assorted cleaning products along with gloves, sponges and a mop.

"Yes," she said. She was halfway to the front when she remembered orange juice. "I'll meet you at the cash register," she said.

She found the orange juice, remembered that she wanted peanut butter, and by the time she finally got to the front of the store, her *husband* was hugging another woman.

To be fair, he was being hugged by the woman ahead of him. She had her arms wrapped tight around his neck with her breasts pushed up against his chest. His arms were down at his sides. She watched as he stepped back, breaking contact. He couldn't go far. There was a cart behind him and the older woman steering it was grossly engaged in what was going on ahead of her.

Chase made use of what space he had and he and the woman were no longer touching.

The cashier, wearing a black T-shirt and jeans, was watching everything. She had a little smile on her well-lined face.

The woman who'd been hugging Chase wasn't smiling. She had her lower lip extended. She was pretty, Raney thought. A little too made-up, perhaps, for a morning grocery store run. Foundation, blush, eyeliner, the whole bit. Her dark hair was perfectly straight and worn in an angled cut around her face. She had on tan linen pants and a matching jacket with heels that made her tall enough to almost look Chase in the eye.

Raney felt short and oddly inadequate in her cotton skirt and casual shirt.

"Don't I at least get a hug after all this time?" the woman asked.

Chase looked over his shoulder, saw Raney and motioned for her to come. She excused herself and stepped in front of the shopper behind Chase. He wrapped an arm around her shoulders. "Sheila, this is my wife, Raney," he said. "Raney, Sheila Stanton. We went to high school together."

The woman tilted her chin down. "Wife?" she repeated. "Terri from the bakery told me you were back. She didn't say anything about a wife."

"Raney was sleeping in while I got pastries," Chase said.

"You're not wearing a ring."

"Both of ours are getting sized. We're just newlyweds," Chase answered.

Sheila finally looked Raney in the eye. "Congratulations."

She didn't sound as if she meant it.

"Well, I should be going," Sheila said, grabbing the plastic sack that the cashier was holding out in her direction.

She was barely out the door when the cashier started laughing, a low chuckle that didn't show any signs of ending soon.

"What?" Chase asked. He was looking out the big front window of the store. When he turned, he looked as if he was ready to strangle someone.

"I saw her sitting in her vehicle when I came into work an hour ago. I wondered what the hell she was up to. I guess she was waiting for you because you hadn't been here three minutes when she suddenly came in."

Chase pulled out his billfold and Raney thought about what he'd told her the previous night about how news traveled in a small town. Sheila had gotten word that Chase was back, had made a logical assumption that he'd need to get groceries at some point and staked out the location.

It wasn't noon yet and she already had her fill of crazy for the week. Chase appeared to be thinking the same thing.

He didn't say another word while they were getting checked out. They had the groceries in the SUV and were belted in before he looked at her. "Sorry about that," he said.

"Somebody you knew well?"

"We dated off and on for a few years after high school. Got arrested with her one night," he added with a smile.

"Arrested? What did you do?"

"A little misunderstanding about some drag racing. Charges were dropped when the cop realized it was Sheila in the car with me. Her dad was the mayor."

She laughed. "I'm beginning to think that you had quite a reputation when you lived here," she said. "I'm married to the local bad boy."

He smiled at her. "Does that make you the new bad girl?"

The minute he said it, he seemed to realize how suggestive it sounded. "Sorry," he said.

The old Raney, with the mousy-brown hair, would have politely ignored it. Looked in the other direction. Not so with the new platinum blonde Raney. Her mind was suddenly fixated on what she might do to earn a reputation.

And almost every thought that came to mind had Chase Hollister playing a predominant role. Her face felt warm. "I guess I've always wondered what it would be like to have my reputation precede me."

He stared at her. His eyes were dark. Sexy.

But like her hair, her courage was new and obviously fleeting. She swallowed hard. "We should go home. The groceries are getting warm."

GROCERIES WEREN'T THE only things getting warm, Chase thought as he drove to the house. Sometimes his mouth was a step ahead of his brain. Certainly suggesting to Raney that he was interested in a bad girl was evidence of that.

He was supposed to be protecting her.

But who was going to protect him from the crazy connection he seemed to feel every time she was within three feet? Truth be told, it had nothing to do with physical distance. She'd been upstairs last night and he'd lain on the couch, wanting her with a vengeance. Even the ache in his leg hadn't been able to shift his focus.

He'd known her for less than twenty-four hours but when he talked to her, it was as if they'd been friends for a lifetime. He couldn't recall ever having a reaction like that to any woman.

This morning, Sheila had surprised him. When they'd dated, it had been an intensely physical relationship. Truth be told, that was about all it had been. As a nineteen-year-old boy, that had been just perfect. He'd always figured she was looking for the same thing. She hadn't made any big scene when he'd left, although after moving with Cal to St. Louis, his brother had told him a couple times that he'd seen Sheila outside of their apartment. Chase had dismissed Cal's comments, assuming he was seeing things.

But then about five years ago he'd gotten an anonymous letter, calling him every name in the book. And while there was nothing overtly connecting it to Sheila, there was something about the sentences, the disparate thoughts that ran together, that reminded him of the woman.

It hadn't been threatening and he'd basically ignored it. By that time, he was hip deep in catching bad guys and didn't have time to worry about hate mail.

But now, the cashier's chuckle ringing in his ears, he wondered if he'd missed something with Sheila.

He and Raney would just need to stay clear of her.

When they got home, he asked Raney to stay in the car while he checked the house. He didn't expect Lloyd to have come back, but he wasn't taking any chances.

The place was clear and if anything, looked even more dismal in the daylight than it had last night. They carried the groceries in but before he put them away, he made good on his promise to toss everything that was in the refrigerator. He dumped a liberal amount of ammonia into a clean bowl, added some water and wiped out the appliance. When he was done, he realized that Raney was wiping down the stove.

"You don't have to clean," he said. "I'll get it."

"Don't be ridiculous," she said. "What am I going to do, watch you?"

"It's not your mess," he said.

"Yeah, but it's my house for a while."

He ran his hands through his hair. "I'm guessing your last safe house was in better shape."

She looked at the trash-strewn counters, the table laden with papers and dirty dishes, the floor that her sandals were sticking to. "You got one thing going for you."

"Really?"

"Yeah. Nobody's shot at me yet today."

He stared at her for a long minute, then a slight smile crossed his face. "The day's early," he said.

She slapped a sponge in his hand. "Got to love an optimist."

Chapter Five

Toward evening, they drove to Hamerton. They hadn't gotten very far before Raney, her face toward the window, said, "I didn't expect it to look like this. It was dark when we came in last night and I guess I didn't fully appreciate it."

Chase glanced across the countryside. They were on a two-lane highway with cornfields on both sides. One of the farmers was more industrious than the other, evidently, because his crop was freshly picked. The trees were just starting to turn. "In a couple weeks, these trees will be really pretty. People come from all over to see the fall colors."

"When they told me I was going to Missouri, I thought Midwest, which made me think flat. And I wasn't expecting all these trees."

"We're far enough south of St. Louis that if you slip up and say you're in the South, nobody will throw green tomatoes at you. And the heavily wooded areas, all part of the Mark Twain National Forest."

"Did you camp around here?"

He had. It was another thing that had changed once his dad died. "Yeah."

"I've never been camping. It seems as if it would be fun."

He studied her. "At the risk of generalizing, the women I've known have associated camping with being wet, cold, hungry and bitten up by mosquitos. That was before we got into the discussion about the possibility of snakes."

"None of that sounds nice, so maybe I've romanticized the idea in my head. I was thinking of hiking the trails during the day. I'd have on cool boots and one of those insulated vests with lots of pockets that would make it look as if I knew what I was doing. Oh, yeah, I'd have a walking stick, too. I always wanted an excuse to use one of those. At night, I'd sit around a big campfire wrapped in a blanket and eat marshmallows. There are no snakes in my camping world."

He laughed. "Maybe when this is all over, you can come back here for a week and give it a try."

"When this is all over," she repeated, her voice more serious. "That has a nice ring."

"A month," he said.

"Seems like forever."

"It'll go faster than you think," he said, hoping it was true. Right now, a month in Ravesville sounded like a very long time. But it would take every bit of that to get the house ready to sell.

They drove another ten miles, to the outskirts of Hamerton where the big box stores were located. They wandered around the store, getting sheets, a coffeepot, more cleaning supplies, and finally ended up in the paint aisle. Chase picked up six gallons of Eggshell White and put them in the cart. Raney did not say anything.

"Don't give me that look," he said.

"What look?"

"The look as if you just lost your dog."

She shook her head. "I don't have a dog."

"Neutral walls. Ask anybody. Neutrals sell."

"Maybe in a five-year-old ranch, but not in a hundred-year-old farmhouse." She continued to walk.

He stopped the cart. "I'm not going to hear the end of this, am I?"

She turned around to look at him. "Don't be ridiculous. I'm not the one talking about it."

He whipped the cart around, unloaded the Eggshell White and waved toward the wall of paint samples. "You've got five minutes."

She skipped back to him. "To pick or to pick and have it mixed?"

"Five minutes."

It ended up being a total of seventeen minutes but he walked out with two gallons of Toasted Meringue, two of Prickly Pear Delight and two of Sunset Wonder. "These are ridiculous names for paint. Why can't they simply call it Sort of Yellow, Pale Green and Orange Red?"

"Because those are boring."

"Uh-huh." They unloaded everything into the car and got buckled in. "Are you hungry?" he asked.

"I could eat. I guess I worked up an appetite this afternoon."

She'd worked hard. They'd made good progress on the kitchen and then she'd gone upstairs to clean the bathroom while he'd walked outside. There, in the corner of the porch, had been a chain saw, which made him think that Brick had probably intended to do the bushes after he got home from his doctor's appointment.

Chase had ruthlessly gone after the big bushes that were crowding the house, not wanting to give anybody with bad intent an opportunity to get close without being seen or worse yet, a place to hide.

Now he had a hell of a pile of brush that he didn't have any idea what to do with. Maybe he should burn it. Wait for a windy day, strike a match, and maybe the house would go, too. Save everybody a whole lot of trouble.

But then he'd have to find another place for Raney and he wasn't sure how that would go. As crazy as it seemed, she was settling in at the old place.

"That looks like a steak house," he said, pointing off to his left. "Does your enjoyment of red meat extend beyond the hamburger?"

"I'm fond of medium-rare filets with sautéed mushrooms."

"Excellent." He pulled in and they got out. "Let me go in first," he said.

"Okay," she said, her tone letting him know that she thought it was kind of unnecessary. "I really doubt that somebody is inside just in the off hopes that we might stop in for dinner." She stopped in her tracks, very dramatically. "Wait, I take that back. Maybe there's another old girlfriend in there, who sat in the parking lot all afternoon, chewing off her lipstick, confident that you'd come this way."

He cocked his head. "You're funny, aren't you?" he said drily. He opened the exterior door and motioned for her to wait in the small vestibule, between the inside and outside doors. He went inside.

He did a quick scan. It was crazy but he didn't like leaving her alone for even a minute. He had always had a good sense of these things, and something was telling him that Raney was still in danger.

He stuck his head back into the vestibule. "Looks okay. Six other tables. I didn't recognize anybody. And they have both a six-and a nine-ounce fillet on the menu."

"Do they have flavored vodka?" she asked quickly.

He pulled back. "I have no idea," he said. "Let's go." He held the door open for her. Once the hostess seated them, the waiter approached. He was early twenties and was checking Raney out. Chase could see the appreciation in his eyes. Raney smiled up at him.

The guy greeted them, still looking at Raney. "Evening," he said. "We get a lot of regulars here but I don't think I've seen you before. You live nearby?"

Chase used his foot to give her a quick nudge on the knee. Maybe he needed to buy her a ring sooner than later. "My wife and I just moved to Ravesville," he said, jumping in.

The man finally looked at Chase and he could read the message loud and clear. *Lucky*

son of a bitch. "I don't live too far from there."
He pulled a lighter from his pocket and lit the
small candle in the middle of the table. "What
can I bring you to drink?" he asked.

Raney ordered a chardonnay and Chase ordered an iced tea. No drinking for him. He
was on duty.

The waiter walked away. "I thought you
were interested in vodka."

"No. Not really." She laughed. "Just making
sure that you don't start thinking that you're
always a step ahead of me."

Not to worry. His head felt muddled whenever she was near. He was pretty sure it had
something to do with her scent and the way
she crossed her legs at the ankles, like a lady.

Which was a bit at odds with some of the
other clues that he was getting. Muddled, for
sure.

"I'm going to wash my hands," Raney said,
pushing her chair back.

Chase almost said that he'd check the bathroom first but decided that really was going
too far. "Okay."

While she was gone, his cell phone buzzed.
He looked at the text message from Dawson.
He'd done his homework. Lloyd lived on the
other side of Ravesville, about three miles
from their house. About six years ago, he'd

been arrested several times for shoplifting and public intoxication. He'd spent some time in jail because he'd failed to show up for his court dates and a warrant had been put out for his arrest. He'd never married and there was no record of children. His work record was spotty up until a few years ago when he started working for Fitzler Roofing.

Well, that answered one question. Mr. Fitzler's company was still going strong. He'd either sold it to someone and they'd kept the name or maybe one of the daughters was running it.

When Raney got back, they ordered. And when the food was delivered, the steaks were cooked just perfect. They ate, both skipped dessert and by the time they were out of the restaurant, it was already dark.

"Tired?" he asked as they settled in for the half-hour drive home.

"A little," she admitted. "I haven't been sleeping all that well lately."

"It will all be over soon," he said, thinking of Harry Malone's upcoming trial.

"I suppose," she said.

He glanced over at her. "You don't sound convinced."

"I'm conflicted."

"Conflicted," he repeated. "Testifying against

Harry Malone is the right thing to do," he said, his tone adamant.

She waved a hand. "I know that. I'm conflicted because I can't help feeling that there was a reason that I got away. I mean, three other women died at his hand. Those are the ones we know about. But I didn't. I lived to tell about it." She turned to him. "Why me?"

Her tone gripped him, making his chest feel heavy. He didn't know what to tell her. "I don't know," he said.

"Maybe I have unfinished business," she said. "Maybe I'm supposed to accomplish something significant. Something that will make a difference."

"Maybe," he said.

"Well, that doesn't make any sense," she said. "I'm not going to discover the cure for cancer or anything remotely close. I'm a career counselor. That's it."

"You probably help people all the time. With their career, right?" he added, a little lamely. "You have an important job."

"'Had,' you mean? I suspect they're going to have to fill my spot."

She didn't sound angry, more resigned if anything. "Are there other jobs for career counselors?" he asked.

"I suppose. It's just that I really loved my

work at Next Steps. I worked almost exclusively with young people—many of whom dropped out of school only to discover that there are very few opportunities for someone with no credentials. They can't even qualify for entry-level positions."

"Pretty shortsighted, right?"

"Sure. But there are always lots of contributing factors. I've seen everything from learning disabilities to teen pregnancy to homelessness to jail."

"You work with ex-cons?"

"Sure. Sometimes I work with the currently incarcerated, depending on when they are going to be released."

"And you visit them in jail? Prison?"

She chuckled, her head leaning back. "Well, they can't exactly come to me."

"That could be pretty dangerous. There are bad people in jail and prison. That's what got them there."

"I know." She turned her head to look at him. "But in my case, it's the classic example of the person you least expect being the person who is going to cause you the trouble. Harry Malone has never been incarcerated. He has a fine reputation."

"That's going to change," he said. He didn't

want her focused on Malone. "Tell me more about your job. What is it that you do exactly?"

"It depends on the client. For those that are new to the program, it might be getting them enrolled in a GED program and helping them develop the confidence and the study skills to be successful. For those further along, who are looking for a job, I work on their soft skills and teach them what most of us intuitively knew when we entered the workforce."

"Like?" Did she realize how her voice lit up when she talked about her work?

"Like how to have a conversation, a real conversation. Many of the clients I work with have been talked *at*, not talked with, and they've developed a response pattern that doesn't help them much in a job interview. They need help on what to wear and help on answering questions about why there are gaps in their employment because they were in jail. That kind of thing."

"I'll bet you're good at it," he said.

"I am. I was," she added, after a few seconds.

"You will be again," he said.

She didn't answer. It made him crazy that some dirtbag had caused this. She'd been tormented for days and now the nightmare was continuing. It wasn't fair.

But life rarely was.

He'd learned that the hard way the first time Brick had taken a belt to him. And when he'd gotten strong enough that he could challenge Brick, the man had been smart enough to change tactics.

And then Chase had had the very real worry that either his mother or Cal wouldn't survive Brick's next episode. So he'd done the only thing he could.

When they pulled into the drive, nothing looked disturbed. He realized that Raney had fallen asleep. He gave her shoulder a gentle shake. "We're home," he said.

She gave him a couple slow blinks. "I'll just sleep out here," she said. "In the car." She closed her eyes again.

"I don't think so." He got out, walked around the car and opened her door. He held out his hand.

She took it. Her skin was warm and soft and so absolutely feminine. He gave her arm a gentle tug and she stood up, a little unsteady. He put his hands on her waist.

Her hair smelled like raspberries and without thought, he raised one hand and touched the very tips. "This surprised me," he admitted. "But I like it. It's cute. Sexy," he added.

She tilted her chin up. Her lips were close. So close. And he desperately wanted to kiss her.

He bent his head.

She closed her eyes.

And then he saw the reflection of lights on the road and heard a car engine. He watched. It turned into the Fitzlers' lane.

This time.

What the hell was he thinking? He'd said he would protect her, had promised that he could keep her safe.

"Chase?" she whispered, her eyes now wide-open.

"I'm tired, Raney. Let's get inside now."

RANEY WAS EXHAUSTED but still her body felt hot and needy. She'd torn open the packaging on her sheets and quickly put them on the mattress. Then she shucked her clothes and climbed in.

Chase had almost kissed her. And she had definitely wanted him to. How the hell she was going to pretend tomorrow that nothing had changed was beyond her.

She needed sleep.

Which was easier than admitting she needed sex.

As tired as she was, she tossed and turned and once when she woke up, she heard noises downstairs. Her heart started beating fast and she looked at the window. Then she heard the sounds of old pipes. Water running. As quietly as she could, she crossed the room and eased the door open.

The lights were on downstairs and Chase, wearing just blue jeans, low on his hips, was using a sponge mop to clean the living room floor. It was one of those fake wooden floors that people wanted to believe looked like wood but it never did. She watched for several minutes, enjoying the show. His biceps flexed with the effort, the strong muscles in his back rippling.

He was working hard. When he shifted, she got a glimpse of the sweat on his chest.

She could feel her own body get warm.

She supposed it was possible that he simply couldn't abide a dirty floor. But somehow she didn't think so. It was much more likely that Chase was having a little troubling sleeping, too, and he was taking it out on the unsuspecting laminate.

She stepped back, closing the door. She returned to her bed and stared into the darkness. What the hell was happening between her and Chase Hollister?

The old Raney would have been intrigued

but likely too shy to do much about it. Blonde Raney? She wasn't sure.

The only thing she was confident of was that it was strangely comforting to know that Chase was losing a little sleep over her.

CHASE WAS SITTING at the kitchen table when Raney got downstairs the next morning. Like last night, still in his blue jeans. But this morning, he'd put on a shirt. He was drinking a cup of coffee and there was a bowl and a cereal box next to it.

"Morning," he said.

"Good morning."

"Sleep well?"

"Pretty good," she said. "How about you?"

He shrugged. "Good enough."

Uh-huh. She poured herself a cup of coffee and sat across from him. "The living room floor looks great," she said. "Did you mop it?"

He stared at the back of the cereal box, as if it was the most interesting thing he'd ever read. "Yeah, I got an early start."

She thought about calling him out but decided there was little to be gained. If he wanted to pretend that their *little moment* outside the prior evening had meant nothing, so be it.

"I thought I might work upstairs some more today," she said.

"I really hate that you're getting sucked into cleaning this place," he said.

"Don't worry about it. It fills the time. At the last place, all I did was watch television. If I see another *Friends* rerun, it won't be pretty. What are your plans?"

"More outside work. I'll probably mow the grass first, then take a look at the roof."

"Do you know how to fix that?" He was a cop, not a carpenter.

"I'm pretty good with my hands," he said.

She let his words hang in the air. "Really?" she said. She stared at his blunt male fingers that were wrapped around his coffee cup. His nails were clipped short.

Capable hands.

Capable of what? Her imagination was running wild. She could see him cupping her breast, judging the weight, running his index finger over her nipple.

She felt hot.

She should retreat.

That would have been BHM.

Now she gathered her courage, channeled blonde Raney and looked him in the eye. "That's good to know," she said, her tone perfectly level. Then she turned on her heel and escaped upstairs.

TEN MINUTES LATER, when Chase sharply turned the wheel of the old riding lawn mower, he was still thinking about the look she'd given him. He made another pass across the ratty yard, his mind reliving every moment in the kitchen.

He was tired. Had given up all pretense of sleep around two and had started mopping the floor. He'd been quiet and Raney had slept through it. Safe in her bed. Alone.

He'd been this close to kissing her the night before. Standing beside the car, with the moonlight washing over them, the urge had been overwhelming. If the other vehicle hadn't come along, he'd have made a big mistake.

He was going to keep his distance.

They had a month. How hard could it be? It wasn't as if there wasn't anything for him to do. After he'd finished mopping the floor, he'd made a list, trying to prioritize the work. If he had to be in Ravesville, he intended to get the house ready to sell.

While the weather was good, he should work outside. There was absolutely no curb appeal. He needed to trim bushes and trees and mow the grass. The front steps needed to be fixed and the roof was a must. In fact, the roof was probably the priority. He shouldn't do anything inside until he was sure that when it rained, the water wasn't going to come flowing down upon newly painted walls.

When he'd told Raney this morning that he thought he could fix the roof, he hadn't been bragging. That was how he'd gotten to know Gordy Fitzler. His neighbor was a roofer, the only one in Ravesville. It had been a godsend for Chase when Old Man Fitzler, as the boys he hired liked to call him, had offered Chase a spot on his summer crew.

He'd taught Chase how to scramble across a roof without losing his balance, how to use a nail gun and how to keep a packet of shingles, weighing a hundred pounds, from shifting on you as you went up the ladder so that you didn't end up in the rose bush thirty feet below.

He'd put on roofs in the blazing sun, which had been painfully intensified by Missouri's high humidity, for two summers. Today, the late-September weather was about perfect for roof work. The sky was a clear blue and the morning temp was a cool sixty with an expected high of seventy-eight.

He walked to the two-car attached garage that sat fifty yards west of the house. When he opened the side door, the smell of mustiness, in sharp contrast to the clear, clean air outside, hit him hard. As expected, there was a lawn mower. Some tools, too. A few shovels and spades stacked in a corner. In addition to that, the building was full of boxes that had not been totally spared from the elements. He glanced upward and wasn't surprised when he saw spots on the ceiling that indicated the garage roof was likely leaking, the same as the house roof.

There were stacks and stacks of newspapers. He suspected they were condo living quarters for any number of rodents. There were balls of snarled-up twine, as if Brick had saved every piece he'd encountered for the past seventy years. Empty coffee cans filled with rusted, bent nails and screws and nuts and bolts. Nothing besides the lawn mower, which appeared in decent shape, looked as if it had been touched for many years.

What the hell had Brick done all day? Shaking his head, Chase grabbed a ladder that hung on the far wall. He tucked it under his arm and left the building. He'd tackle the garage another day.

Ten minutes later, he was on the roof, surveying the damage. It was no wonder that there was water damage inside the house. The shingles were old and brittle and their edges were lifted, allowing water to seep under. In several small areas, the shingles were missing altogether, probably due to severe wind.

He realized, rather disheartened, that rather than a few quick repairs, the house really needed a new roof. He supposed he had a choice. He could nail down what was there the best he could and then pick up a couple packets of shingles at one of the big box stores for the missing sections. The new ones wouldn't match the old ones and it would look like hell, but at least the roof wouldn't leak. It would get him and Raney by for the time being. Then, when he and his brothers listed the house, they could price it lower than market, to make up for the fact that the buyer would need to install the new roof.

Or he could put a new roof on. Which was a hell of a lot of work. Working alone, it would take weeks.

He'd be on the roof; Raney would be inside.

Distance. That was what he'd told himself was the answer.

He was halfway down the ladder when he heard the sound of an approaching car. He twisted to see the road.

Chapter Six

It was an old pickup, maroon with white lettering on the door. He smiled. He remembered that truck from when it was brand-new. Had driven it a couple times with a firm warning not to get it scratched up ringing in his ears.

The truck turned into the lane. Chase waited until it came to a stop and the old man driving it slowly climbed out. Gordy Fitzler's hair was thin and completely white and he looked thinner than Chase remembered. He approached, extending his hand. "Mr. Fitzler," Chase said.

The man made a scoffing noise. "It's been a long time, Chase, but there's no need for formality. Call me Gordy or Old Man, the way you used to."

"Didn't know you knew that we called you that," Chase admitted.

"Made me laugh every time I heard it. You and your friends were forty years younger than me and I could still work circles around you.

I thought I saw lights here the other night and then this morning when I was having coffee in town, I heard you were back."

"Just to get the house ready to sell," Chase corrected.

"You'll have your hands full with that, I suspect." Gordy looked at the ladder that was leaning up against the house. "Brick should have redone his roof years ago."

"Just discovered that. You're not still getting up on roofs, are you?" Chase asked.

Gordy shook his head. "Retired for many years. My old knees couldn't take it anymore. But my son-in-law took over. Jonah's doing a good job. He could get you what you need and probably drop it off this afternoon."

Chase didn't bother to ask about the price. He knew it would be fair. "How is your wife?"

Gordy shook his head. "Glenda's been gone now for almost two years."

"I'm sorry. I didn't know."

"Figured as much. Suspected that Brick didn't keep you up-to-date on the news. You know, Lloyd Doogan works for my son-in-law."

"How's he do?"

"Okay. Works hard when he's there. Has a few demons that chase him once in a while."

Hard to tell what he suffered as a child. And

if there was anyone in Ravesville who knew the truth about Brick Doogan, it was Gordy. He'd been witness to the assorted bruises and other injuries that Chase had shown up with. It was probably why he'd offered him a spot on his couch whenever Chase had been desperate enough to knock on the door.

"Tell me about those demons," Chase said.

Gordy shrugged. "I don't know all the details. Just know that every once in a while, he'll get into the sauce and be too hungover to climb on top of a roof. Anyway, I heard you got a wife."

"Raney," Chase said, feeling bad that he was lying to Gordy. But Raney's safety was more important. "She's inside."

"I'd like to meet her."

"Of course." They walked up the porch, him pointing out the spots that Gordy should avoid. He opened the door. There was no sign of Raney.

"Raney," he called out. "There's a friend here who'd like to meet you."

She walked out of the kitchen, a towel over her shoulder. She'd put on old jeans that molded to her firm body and a light gray V-neck T-shirt. She looked at him, then Gordy. "Good morning," she said.

"Ma'am," Gordy said, extending his hand.

"I'm Gordy Fitzler. I wanted to offer my congratulations. You got yourself a good one here."

Raney smiled. "I know," she said, playing her part perfectly. "It's a pleasure to meet you."

"I'm just the next house down the road. You ever need anything, just stop by."

"I will," she said.

"The roof is worse than I thought," Chase said. "It needs to be replaced. Gordy's son-in-law will drop some shingles by this afternoon so that I can get started on the work."

"Sounds like a big job," she said.

"He knows what he's doing. Best roofer I ever had," Gordy added. "Now, don't be a stranger," he said, turning to leave.

Chase walked the man to his truck and made sure he got off okay. Then he went back inside. Raney was standing at the window. "Sweet guy," she said.

Gordy had had high expectations, hadn't tolerated any backtalk and had restored Chase's faith that a man didn't have to yell to have himself be heard. "Yeah."

He suddenly found himself wanting to tell Raney about Brick Doogan, about the crazy things the man had done and about how he used to fantasize that his mother had married Gordy Fitzler instead.

He'd forgiven his mother. For letting it happen. For choosing to ignore it. For not being stronger. He'd forgiven her because she'd finally asked him to. She'd been on her deathbed and it was the only peace he could offer her.

But those weren't things he talked about. To anyone. Especially not someone who was just passing through his life.

"I'm going to start tearing off shingles," he said and walked out the door.

Two hours later, he was still on the roof ripping off shingles when he heard the front door open. He looked down. Raney had changed her clothes and was wearing a skirt that showed off her pretty legs and a shirt that showed off her other assets.

Distance, he reminded himself.

"Hey," she said, looking up and shading her eyes with the palm of her hand. "I thought I might make spaghetti for dinner but I forgot to buy Italian seasoning yesterday. Can I borrow your SUV to run into town?"

"I'll go with you," he said, starting to climb down.

"Do you really think that's necessary? You said yourself that no one has any reason to believe that Raney Hollister is Lorraine Taylor. Nothing is going to happen."

He stopped, halfway down. Distance. She

was right. It was safe. And they should act as normally as possible. Which meant that one of them could run to the store without the other.

"Okay," he said. "Keys are on the counter."

"Want anything else?"

"Yeah. Some really good bread from the bakery."

"Got it," she said. "Try not to fall off the roof while I'm gone," she teased. She seemed more lighthearted. It made him realize that she was probably really glad to have the freedom to leave the house, to do something as mundane as grocery shopping after having been confined to the house in Miami.

A few minutes later, the SUV pulled out of the driveway. He watched it until it turned the corner, no longer in view. He checked the time on his watch and then went back to pulling up shingles.

The next time he checked his watch, it was a half hour later. Raney should be home soon. He used the back of his arm to wipe away the sweat gathering on his forehead. Damn, it was hot. He should probably get some water.

He got down and drank two big glasses, standing at the living room window, watching the road. What the hell was taking her so long?

Ten minutes later he was really worried.

He tried her cell phone but she didn't pick up.

Moving quickly, he put his gun in the small of his back and slipped on a loose shirt. He rubbed his thigh, hating that his climbing up and down the ladder and crab-walking around the roof were taking a toll on his injured muscle.

Before he'd been hurt, he'd regularly jogged. The mile and a half into town would have been nothing. But he hadn't run for six weeks. When the doc had given him the release to return to active duty, he'd suggested he lay off vigorous training for another week or two.

That couldn't be helped now and he wasn't letting it hold him back. He felt an overwhelming need to get to town, fast.

He had just opened the front door when he saw his SUV sedately driving down the road. He watched, and with every damn rotation of the tires, he felt his irritation grow.

She was barely out of the car when he stalked off the front porch.

"Hi," she said, as if there was nothing wrong.

"Where the hell have you been?" he asked, his tone harsher than he intended. He took a deep breath, struggling for the control that generally came so naturally to him.

She frowned at him and held up the plastic bag in her hand. "I went to the store."

"It's a mile and a half," he said. "And the

store has five aisles," he added, sarcasm in his tone. "I called you."

She pulled her cell from her purse, pushed a button. "I'm sorry. I had it on silent."

"What took you so long?"

"I met someone," she said. "The waiter from the restaurant last night."

Little red dots danced at the edge of his vision. "I didn't realize the two of you had set up a rendezvous."

"I… I…" She dropped the bag and small tins of basil and oregano rolled out onto the ground. "What the hell are you talking about?"

"In case you've forgotten, *honey*, you're married. And he knows it, too."

She walked toward him. When she got close enough, she poked him in the chest with her index finger. "You. Are. An. Idiot."

Huh?

"Before I went to the grocery store, I went to the little bookstore on the corner. I forgot to pack any books. And I like to read. Anyway, he was there, looking through a stack of used books. We recognized each other and started talking. He admitted that he was looking for business books, the kind that might help him be prepared for the job interview that he has next week."

"Oh." As responses went, it was pretty inadequate.

And she didn't appear to be inclined to let it go when she repeated, "Oh?" then added, "That's the best you can do?"

Pretty much. He felt like a fool. "I'm sorry," he said. "I was worried when you were gone so long."

Her eyes softened. "I assumed you'd be busy on the roof."

"The house is secondary. My first responsibility is to protect you."

"Don't you think I'm safe here?" she asked.

"You should be," he said. "But a good cop never assumes anything."

"We're meeting again tomorrow," she said.

He felt his emotions spike. "The hell you are."

"He's interviewed for five jobs and hasn't gotten any of them. He knows that he's doing something wrong."

"That's not your concern."

"Of course it isn't. But I have the skills to help him. God knows I have the time," she added.

In her tone, he heard frustration that might have been edging toward bitterness. He remembered hearing the pride in her voice when she'd spoken about her work.

Harry Malone had taken a great deal away from her. And now Chase was about to compound the issue.

He swallowed hard. "I want his name, his address, his previous address. Hell, I want to know his damn shoe size."

She opened her mouth, then shut it without speaking.

"And you'll meet here. Where I can watch him," he added. Wouldn't that be fun? Standing by while the two of them huddled over the idiot's résumé.

Finally she nodded. "Ten," she said.

"Ten what?" he asked, already preparing to go outside where he could hit something. Hard.

"I think he wears a ten. I spent one summer selling shoes. I'm a pretty good judge."

He wanted to laugh. Damn her, he wanted to laugh. "Well, I wear a twelve and if he so much as steps an inch out of line, I'm going to plant it where a foot should never go."

He turned and stalked back toward his ladder.

And finally did let a smile loose when he heard her quiet laughter.

RANEY MADE SPAGHETTI, a big salad and garlic bread for dinner. She let Chase know about a half hour before it was ready so that he could come inside and shower. He'd been working outside all afternoon. The shingles and all the other assorted supplies needed to replace a roof had been delivered midafternoon along with a big Dumpster to catch all the old shingles that he dropped from the roof.

"Smells good," he said when he came in. "Really good."

Raney's stomach did a little flip. It had been a long time since she'd cooked for anyone. "You've got fifteen minutes," she said.

He took eleven. He helped her carry the bowls from the counter to the table. And then he proceeded to eat his way through two platefuls. He finally pushed his plate away. "What else can you cook?" he asked.

She shrugged. "I guess about everything. I was brought up that if you could read, you could cook."

He shook his head. "Not true. I'm a literate man. I can't cook." He pushed his chair back, picked up both their dirty plates and carried them to the sink.

Relaxed, she rested one elbow on the table and used her fingers to play with the ends of her short hair. "I suspect it's that you choose not to cook, not that you can't."

"I've had some spectacular disasters," he

admitted. He turned the faucet on and added dish soap.

"Well, I detest doing dishes. So I'll cook and you'll clean up. This is a marriage that could work," she added.

He turned around, his face much more serious than her casual remark. "Why aren't you married?"

"I... I was." She answered before she considered whether she wanted to have this discussion with him.

A quick look of surprise crossed his face before he managed to shut it down. "I didn't know that."

"Probably didn't get to the fine details in my file. It was short-lived. Just two years. We've been divorced for over five years."

"Does your ex know about Harry Malone?"

"I doubt it. He lives in Hawaii. He surfs. Professionally."

"Let me guess. You didn't want to move to Hawaii?"

She shook her head. "I didn't want to share with his mistress."

Even though she'd known the marriage wasn't working, Mike's duplicity had hit her hard. His training schedule had required them to live apart for long stretches of time. Still, she'd never expected him to cheat. When she'd stumbled upon the note in his pocket, she'd been so angry.

She'd confronted him with it and he had readily admitted that it had been going on for months, leading her to believe that the accidental discovery might not have been so accidental. He'd wanted her to know, wanted to be out of a marriage that he was no longer interested in working at.

The divorce had been fast and as amicable as a divorce could probably be. The ink on the divorce paperwork hadn't been dry before Mike and Lenore were living together.

Raney had thrown herself into her work. And friends had told her not to worry, that she'd meet someone. She'd smiled, neither agreed nor disagreed, but in her lonely bed, she had spent some time wondering if this was it for her. Was she going to be alone?

It was a suddenly chilling thought to think that *this* might be as close to a real marriage as she was going to get.

"He was an idiot," Chase said, his tone hard. His gaze was intense, the set of his jaw stiff. He came back to the table and sat down. His chair was at a right angle to hers and he leaned forward, reached out a hand and touched her arm. The nail on his bare ring finger was bruised, and she suspected he'd hit it with a hammer. His skin was hot. "You know that, right?" he added.

What she knew was that Chase Hollister affected her in a way that no man, even Mike, had ever affected her. He made the nerve endings in her body come alive and almost beg to be touched, stroked, loved.

"It was a long time ago. We were both young."

"No excuse for what he did," Chase said.

And she knew for sure that while Chase might have been the bad boy in his youth, he'd grown into the kind of man who knew right from wrong. He would do the right thing.

He would protect the witness.

He wouldn't cross the line.

Which meant it would be up to her.

But he had the advantage. While he might not know everything, he knew more about her than she did about him. He'd casually brushed off the idea of marriage when they'd discussed it at the café but that didn't mean that he wasn't in a committed relationship. If so, it didn't matter how blond her hair was—she wasn't doing anything about the attraction. Having been on the receiving end of that once, she didn't ever want to cause that kind of pain for someone else. "I know you mentioned some aversion to marriage," she said, deliberately keeping her tone light, "but are you involved with anyone right now?"

He stared at her, his amber eyes intense. His handsome face was even more tanned from his time on the roof. "I'm pretty busy at work," he said.

It was sort of an answer.

"I imagine you are," she murmured.

"I haven't dated anyone for over a year," he added.

Did that mean that he hadn't had sex in over a year? Maybe if her hair was fire-engine red she would be brave enough to ask for clarification.

What did it matter? He'd had the chance to kiss her last night and he'd pulled back. She'd been rejected once before by her ex-husband. It had hurt badly. She wasn't going to put herself in that position again.

She pushed her chair back from the table. "I'm tired," she lied. "I think I'll turn in."

CHASE WANDERED AROUND the downstairs, completely avoiding Brick's room. The only television in the house was in there, but he wasn't that desperate to watch something.

He could start taking off the paint on the woodwork, but that would involve the use of turpentine and the fumes might get bad. He could always open some windows, but that wasn't something he was willing to do at night. He wanted the house closed up tight. A locked door or window wasn't much of a deterrent, but it might buy a second or two and sometimes that was all a person needed.

He should just go to bed and get up really early in the morning to make use of the daylight. But he felt unsettled. He'd made his fourth lap around the house when his cell phone rang. He looked at the number and smiled.

"You still owe me," he answered.

"Of course I do," Bray said. "What's the house look like?"

"It's in pretty rough shape. Needs paint and new carpet most everywhere but that's cosmetic. I'm going to replace the roof. It's leaking in several spots."

"I really wish I could be there to help. But this case is just about to crack. I've been after one of these guys for two years."

"Don't worry about it. We're doing fine."

"We?"

"I'm guarding a witness while I'm here. We needed a safe place to stash her and Ravesville seemed like a good option."

"What's her name?"

"Raney. She's pretending to be my wife."

"Now I really wish I could be there. You've probably got everybody in the town talking about it."

"Speaking of town, I saw Summer Wright."

There was silence on the other end. "Summer Blake, you mean," Bray said, his voice tight.

"Nope. Summer Wright. She's divorced. Not gossip, got it straight from her."

More silence. He gave Bray a full minute more, but he still didn't say anything.

"She's got a couple kids."

"Hey, you know what, I've got another call coming in. Take care of your witness and get that house ready to sell."

Chase stared at his phone. His brother regularly dealt with the dregs of society. Nothing much ruffled him. But hearing Summer Wright's name had practically rendered him speechless.

That was interesting.

He lay down on the lumpy sofa, suddenly feeling better that he'd talked to his brother. He closed his eyes. He got up once in the middle of the night to make sure the house was still secure and to take off his jeans and pull on athletic shorts. It was hot. He did not want to run the air conditioner or even the fan because it could make it difficult to hear an intruder.

When he lay down the second time, he didn't open his eyes again until he heard Raney came downstairs the next morning.

"Morning," she said, her voice husky from sleep.

He shifted to a sitting position. "What time is it?"

"A little after six," she said. "I didn't mean to disturb you."

"No problem," he said. He got up and quickly pulled at the hem of his shorts. He sure as hell didn't want Raney to see the scar on his leg. Didn't want to answer any questions. Didn't want her to have any concerns that he might not be 100 percent.

What he had on was what he wore when he sparred with Dawson at the gym, but suddenly it felt insufficient.

He needed to wear a parka around Raney. Something that zipped, and buttoned, with a little Velcro just in case. Something that would take some time to shed. Something that would give him some time to develop a little perspective.

Right now, he had none. Because she was leaning forward from the waist, looking at the stack of books on the end table, and her little pajama top was gaping at the top, giving him a truly excellent look at her breasts.

She was not wearing a bra.

He could not look away.

But then she straightened up, looking at him. Assessing.

And he lifted his hand.

Chapter Seven

And clamped it down hard on the back of his neck. Holy hell. What was he thinking?

He practically ran to the kitchen, grabbed the empty coffeepot, filled it with water and then completed the whole coffee routine. He didn't turn around until the first drops hit the bottom with a quick sizzle.

She was sitting at the table, as if nothing had happened. Had he imagined it? Was it simply wishful thinking?

Was he losing his mind?

"What time is that guy coming?" he asked, needing something concrete to focus on.

"His name is Keith. He'll be here around eleven. I thought I'd clear off a spot on the dining room table where we could work."

Chase craned his neck to see into the other room. The old wooden table was covered with newspapers and brown sacks and milk cartons that had been emptied and then refilled with water, as if Brick was afraid the well was going out. There were stacks of bath towels at the far end. He suspected they'd been clean at one time but now they had a heavy layer of dust. In the middle, there was a pile of mail, looking as if it had been opened and then just tossed. He supposed he'd have to go through it at some point.

There was a matching china cabinet in the corner that had nothing in it. His mother's dishes, the ones she'd gotten from her mother, chipped and probably full of lead, had been packed away after his mother's death eight years ago. Bray had taken them, said he'd put them in storage. Chase didn't care as long as Brick didn't have them.

It was one of the few things that her sons had gotten from the house. They'd left the furniture, the cabinet, the table and the six wooden chairs, the same color as the table but not quite the same pattern. He could still remember how delighted his mother had been when she'd discovered them at a neighbor's sale. They'd replaced the ones that had come with the table but had fallen apart after three boys and a husband had used them hard.

She'd bought them after his dad had died and before Brick had come into the picture. The idiot had been in the house for less than a year when he'd picked up one of the chairs and thrown it at the china cabinet, cracking the front pane of glass.

The crack was still there.

"I found a couple garbage cans in the garage yesterday," he said. "I'll get them for you."

"No problem," she said. She pushed her chair back, walked over to the coffeepot, getting just close enough that her arm brushed against his bare ribs. "Sorry," she murmured.

He couldn't say anything. Had she done that intentionally?

She moved away. As if it was nothing.

He was pathetic, trying to read something off a blank page. "I'm going outside," he said.

"Did you eat?" she asked, sounding concerned.

There was no way that he could stay in the kitchen. "I'll grab something later," he said. "I want to work while the day is cool."

Outside, he walked to the garage. He'd considered leaving the extension ladder out the night before so that he didn't have to go back into the garage but had discarded that notion immediately. He didn't want to give anyone easy access to the second story of the house, to Raney's room. So he'd stashed the ladder behind some boxes, making it tough for someone to find.

He carried the ladder to the side of the house, tied his tool belt around his waist and started climbing. Fully extended, the ladder was just tall enough for him to reach the roof of the second floor.

Bray and Cal would both be appreciative of his work on the house. They would not second-guess his decision to replace the roof or anything else. They would be grateful that he had taken charge. Cal would not likely say it. Cal never said much to him anymore. Something had changed about the time of his mother's death. There hadn't been a big blow up. Nope. It was as if Cal had just shut down.

They needed to talk about that. But Cal hadn't been around much in the past eight years, and on the rare occasions the two brothers had been together, Chase hadn't wanted to dredge up old issues. He'd settled for stilted conversations and awkward silences. It was past time for that to change, and for the first time in a long time, felt as if now might be the time to press the issue. He and Bray always tried to get together on Thanksgiving. It had been their mother's favorite holiday. There were times when either or both of them had to work on the actual holiday because crime never took a break. In those cases, they had a flexible approach.

It might be on Monday or Tuesday or Wednesday, it didn't matter. It was still Thanksgiving dinner and they did the whole traditional thing. They generally found a place that cooked the turkey and all the trimmings and packed it up all nice and pretty so that the customer could take it home and eat it off real plates.

If the house wasn't sold by Thanksgiving, he could invite Bray here. And Cal, too. He wouldn't take no for an answer.

The idea was oddly appealing.

He got to the top of the ladder, stepped off onto the roof and squatted next to the area where he'd started prying off shingles with his crowbar. By Thanksgiving, the trial would be over. Raney would be home.

He jabbed the edge of the crowbar under the shingle and jerked his arm, sending the old shingle flying. It was a crazy idea to think about celebrating here. The house needed an exorcism, not a family holiday.

CHASE HAD BEEN working outside for more than three hours when he saw an old Toyota Camry drive down the road, slow well before the driveway and make the turn. It was black but filthy with road dust. When Keith got out, with the loose-limbed stride of someone in his early twenties, Chase felt a sharp pain in his thigh that had been dully aching all morning, as if damaged nerve endings had picked that exact moment to wake up.

Dawson's taunt, *You're not getting any younger*, rang in his ears as he sidestepped his way down the steep slant of the roof, caught the top rung of the ladder with his foot and climbed down.

He wasn't, that was true. But then again, at any age, taking a bullet was a kick in the butt. It hadn't helped the head games when the surgeon said that had the bullet been an inch to the right, he'd have probably bled out at the scene. It had been a postsurgery buzzkill that no amount of narcotics had busted through.

After a crappy twenty-four hours, he'd chosen to focus on the positive. It hadn't been an inch to the right and he'd lived to tell about it.

So his leg hurt a little. Big deal. Didn't mean that he was going to sit back and let some punk kid get the best of him. Not on his home territory.

Home. Territory.

Again, crazy thoughts.

It was just that since almost the moment he'd arrived, there'd been something right about being back in this house that he'd sworn he'd never return to. And that had a lot to do with Raney.

Who was about to get cozy with Keith.

Chase slammed the door on his way into the house.

RANEY TOLD HERSELF that she absolutely would not let Chase distract her from the task at hand. She had barely invited Keith into the dining room when Chase stormed into the house, scuffing his boots on the floor, banging cupboard doors and scraping chairs across the floor.

She reviewed Keith's résumé and tried to ignore the noise. Keith showed no reaction to it. After a few minutes of enduring the commotion, she looked up.

"Can I help you with something?" she asked, pitching her voice so that he could hear.

Chase stuck his head around the corner of the doorway. "Don't mind me," he said. He was chewing peanut-butter crackers. Noisily.

She narrowed her eyes at him.

He showed no response, simply pulled his head back. He did, however, quiet down a bit. He did not leave.

What did she care if he wanted to act like a fool? She turned to Keith, smiled and got started. Two hours later, they had discussed potential modifications to his résumé, reviewed his answers to common interview questions, talked about his short-and long-term goals and developed a reasonable plan to get there.

Chase had to be bored out of his mind. He was behaving, though, quietly sitting in the kitchen.

"I do so much better when you're the one asking the questions," Keith said, giving her a big smile. "I need you to be with me at the interview."

A cupboard door slammed. She ignored it.

"I really appreciate all this help," Keith added. "At least let me buy you lunch."

Something hit the floor in the kitchen. Hard. She suspected it might have been the toaster.

Keith, finally catching on, rolled his eyes. "I guess not," he said.

She shook her head, stood up and walked him to the front door. "Let me know how your interview goes," she said.

She waited until his car turned onto the road before turning to find Chase. He was standing at the stove, his back to her, spatula in hand. She was ready to blast him.

Then he turned, still holding the spatula but now also a plate. He'd cooked a grilled-cheese sandwich. "I thought you might be hungry," he said. "You missed lunch."

Oh, good grief. "I thought you didn't cook."

"This isn't cooking. It's survival."

"Thank you," she said.

"He can't really think that 'I was under-utilized' is a good answer for why he only lasted three months at the telemarketing company," Chase said.

"He's Gen Y, like me. We all think we're underutilized. You're Gen X, apples and oranges."

"Thanks for making me feel a hundred years old."

Sexiest hundred-year-old guy she'd ever met. She smiled. "Sorry. Next year I'll be in my thirties. We'll be in the same decade of our lives. If that makes you feel any better," she added.

"Stop, please. In any event, we'll probably both be working for him in ten years."

"I hope not. Didn't you hear that his long-term goal is to own his own restaurant?"

"It'll be great. You can be the short-order cook and I'll be the bouncer at the door."

"Restaurant. Not biker bar." She wiped her mouth on a paper napkin. "That doesn't seem like a great next job for you."

He shrugged. "Always got to be open to the possibilities. Ready to move on to the next opportunity."

She'd been teasing, but now he was serious. She wasn't sure what to say.

"How's the roof coming?" she asked.

"Pretty good."

"Can I take a look?"

He studied her. "I don't think that's a good idea. This is a big two-story house. I'm pretty high in the air. It doesn't bother me but I'm used to it—like Gordy said, I did it for years."

"But I've never seen a roof get put on. If I do get my own house someday, that would be a good thing for me to know. I'm not afraid of heights."

"The first summer that I worked for Gordy, about midway through the season, Brad Morgan, who was a year older than me, made a mistake. A costly one. He fell more than twenty feet. He broke his pelvis and cracked several vertebrae. He was in bad shape. I won't take that chance that you might get injured. And I certainly don't think it's what Chief Bates had in mind when I described this as a safe house."

She wasn't going to be able to budge him. "Oh, fine. Then, I'm going to open the Toasted Meringue and get started in the kitchen. It's the one room where the roof doesn't seem to be leaking."

"You know, I really appreciate everything you're doing in the house."

It was hard to be irritated with him when

he was such a nice guy. "I know you do. I appreciate that I'm not opening Eggshell White."

"I'd have probably woken up one morning and you'd have painted me Eggshell White."

"Maybe." She wanted to talk to him about the house but didn't know exactly how to do it. Her friends who had remodeled their homes were always asking her opinion on things, saying that she had a good eye for color and design. But she didn't think Chase was especially interested. *Neutrals sell.* He was totally focused on that. But she felt compelled to say something.

He had a gem here. It had taken her a little bit to see it. From the minute she'd arrived, she'd loved the outside, with its wide porch and the big windows on both floors. She'd been a little disappointed with the insides, because it was dark and dismal and had so much clutter that it was hard to see past that. But now that she'd had some time to look around, she felt differently.

"Hey, I had a chance to look around this morning while I was waiting for Keith. I needed to make some space for us to work at the dining room table and while I was in there, I happened to take a look under the carpet. It's sort of coming up on that one side." If it hadn't been before, it was now because once she'd spied a small section of the floor, she'd had to see more. "Did you know that there is really lovely hardwood flooring under there? I mean, it needs to be refinished and all that, but it's nice."

"The next owner can refinish floors. For now, I'll get the carpet cleaned and tack down that corner."

She hated the idea of that carpet staying. She knew she wasn't going to be living here but really, it was just a shame to cover beautiful wood like that.

"You know what the living room is missing?" she asked.

He smiled at her. "I have no idea."

"Bookshelves. You could build them into the two corners and that room would pop."

"Pop," he repeated.

"And I'd take those curtains down and put in those shades that you can raise from either the top or the bottom, depending on the time of day and the position of the sun. And it goes without saying that flooring in there, which is intended to look like wood but doesn't, would need to go. But you could probably find something that would closely match the wood in the dining room."

"Which will be covered by carpet. No bookshelves," he added. "I will take the curtains down only because they smell, but the next owner can do his or her own windows. I'm not decorating. Refurbishing. Or gentrifying," he added.

"But you're sort of flipping. I mean, I realize you didn't buy this house with the intent of fixing it up and selling it to make a nice profit but you did inherit it, it needs to be fixed up and you *could* make a nice profit."

"I want a quick sale. That's more important to me." Chase pushed his chair back. "Speaking of which, I better get busy. I may need to run into town this afternoon. I'm almost out of nails."

She was disappointed that she hadn't been able to get him to see the possibilities in the house. But it really wasn't her worry. "I'd be happy to do the nail run. I forgot to buy oatmeal yesterday and I want to make some granola."

She could tell that he wanted to say no. But he probably felt bad about not letting her on the roof and shutting down her decorating pleas. "Okay. I guess there's no reason to think there's any risk."

A HALF HOUR LATER, Raney had her oatmeal and two bags of chips, because it did seem as if Chase went through them at an alarming rate. As she drove down the street, she saw that the big church on the corner was having a car wash to raise money to assist with the winter heating bills of the elderly. There was a line of cars that stretched around the block, waiting to be washed.

None of them looked that dirty.

Small towns were certainly interesting. A hundred feet from the Wright Here, Wright Now Café, she made the decision to stop. She wouldn't stay long but she was thirsty and an iced tea would do the trick. The weather was changing. Late morning, when she'd been working with Keith, it had been comfortably warm and sunny. But now it was hot and very humid. The wind was picking up.

She wondered if a storm was headed in their direction. She definitely shouldn't stay long at the café. Chase would need all the nails he could get in hopes of having the roof patched before the rain hit.

Raney opened the café door. Summer was behind the counter and she looked up and smiled. "Hi, Raney. Nice to see you again."

Raney took a stool at the counter. It was well past lunchtime and only two booths had customers. She eyed the pie case on the back counter. "Is that lemon meringue?" she asked.

Summer nodded. "Made fresh this morning."

"I'll take one," she said. If Chase could see this, he'd probably make some crack about her falling off the healthy-eater wagon. He liked to tease her.

That was what she'd been doing this morning. Teasing him. When she'd woken up, blonde Raney had taken over. Instead of getting dressed, she'd come downstairs in her pajamas. And then she'd gotten even bolder and deliberately leaned over to look at the books, knowing that he'd be able to see down her shirt.

He'd looked. And when he'd raised his hand and she'd thought he was going to touch her, she'd about melted.

But then he'd double-timed it to the kitchen. The image of what might have been had given her the courage to brush up against him.

His skin had been very warm. And he'd been very sexy with his bare chest and shorts.

But he'd left the kitchen quickly, as if he couldn't wait to get away from her. Blonde Raney had struck out.

Which was a silly thought because there was a distinct possibility that blonde Raney was all talk and no action. That, when push came to shove, if Chase was interested, she'd be the one running for the door. Her inexperience would catch up with her.

She'd dated Mike for three years before she'd married him three weeks after graduating from college. Two years later, at age twenty-four, she was already divorced. A divorcée.

Gun-shy. She'd made a mistake about Mike and that had caused her to question her judgment skills. And she'd chosen to play it safe for the past five years. But now, a month past her twenty-ninth birthday, that wasn't feeling right anymore.

Harry Malone had changed things. Sure. But this was even more than making good on a terrified promise in the dark that if she ever got away, she was going to live. Really live.

Even more because Chase Hollister heated her blood like nobody else had for a very long time.

The man was gorgeous, and sex appeal hung tight to his very nice rear end and broad shoulders. She ached to touch him.

The door to the café opened and Sheila Stanton walked in. She made eye contact with Raney and sat at the counter, one empty stool between them.

There was absolutely no reason to not be polite to her. Other than that she'd had her arms wrapped around Chase's neck. But Raney had been raised to be the bigger person. And Chase had left the grocery store with her, not Sheila. "Hi," Raney said.

Sheila smiled without showing any teeth. She ordered coffee but didn't touch it once Summer had poured it. Instead, she turned to look at Raney. "Where's that handsome husband of yours?"

"Home. Working on the house."

"Where was it that you two met?"

A skitter of alarm ran through her. She and Chase hadn't really practiced their story. "We met in St. Louis," she said. "Mutual friends introduced us."

"And what is it that you do there?"

She thought of Chase's comments of how information flowed in a small town. "Adult education," Raney lied. It was close enough to the truth that if Sheila happened to hear about the help she'd offered to Keith, the story should hold.

Raney opened her purse, pulled out some bills and looked for Summer. She was at the far end of the restaurant, leaning over a booth, wiping down the table. Her shirt had come untucked in the back and Raney could see a couple inches of smooth skin.

Holy hell. What was that? Summer had a bruise the size of a baseball on her lower back.

Not fresh but rather the purple and green of an injury that had occurred sometime earlier.

She could feel the pie in her stomach start to roll. She'd had bruises like that after her encounter with Harry Malone. She straightened up when her ribs began their familiar ache.

Almost as if Summer could sense Raney's inspection, she stood straight, pulling her shirt down self-consciously. She turned and made eye contact with Raney.

There was a plea in Summer's eyes. For what, Raney had no idea. *Please don't tell anyone what you saw. Please don't ask me how I got it. Please help me.*

Raney quickly checked to see if Sheila had also been looking, but the woman was punching keys on her smartphone. Raney turned on her stool, just slightly, and mouthed the words, "Do you want to talk?"

Summer shook her head. Sharply. Definitively.

Okay, she wasn't asking for help. Raney had to assume it was one of the other choices. Perhaps Summer had fallen or run into something. Raney knew the possibility of that was slim. The woman had been beaten. But by who?

Her ex-husband? Was that what had sparked Summer's unfavorable response to the man that first morning that Raney and Chase had eaten breakfast at the Wright Here, Wright Now Café? But surely they'd been separated for some time if the divorce was already finalized. The bruise was old but not that old.

She understood the woman's reluctance to talk about it. After Harry Malone...well, she'd *had* to talk about it. The police had been relentless in their questioning. But every damn conversation had been painful, so painful.

When Summer was behind the counter, Raney pushed a twenty in her direction. "Thanks," she said, not waiting for change. "See you soon."

When she got back in her SUV, it was sticky hot, the black leather interior almost burning her bare legs. She turned the key, flipped on the air conditioner and put on her sunglasses.

She was halfway home and she still hadn't decided whether to tell Chase about what she'd seen. What would he say? "Mind your own business"? "We have our own problems"? She didn't think so. He would encourage Summer to make a police report. But her ex was a cop. What a mess.

She saw a dark car approaching fast from behind. The road was narrow, and up ahead, it was double-striped, indicating a no-passing zone. She slowed, thinking she'd let it squeeze by now. She saw it move to the other lane and figured it would zip past her.

It got parallel and she caught a glimpse inside right before the driver cranked the wheel, making the vehicle swerve sharply toward her.

Raney jerked her own wheel. She felt her front right tire drop off the road, and suddenly she was rolling. She felt her head hit something and suddenly, she felt nothing at all.

Chapter Eight

Chase had sixteen nails left when he heard the rumble of an engine. He looked down and recognized Lloyd Doogan's old motorcycle. He was going very fast, and when he turned onto the lane leading up to the house, his back tire slid on the loose gravel.

What the hell? Chase was off the roof and down the ladder in seconds.

"You've got to come quick," Lloyd said. He was wringing his hands.

"What's wrong, Lloyd?" Chase asked.

"Your wife, that woman, she's hurt."

Chase felt his chest tighten up. "Raney?" he said. "Raney is hurt?"

"Yes. On the road."

Chase dropped his nail gun. In two strides he reached Lloyd's motorcycle. "We're taking this and I'm driving."

Less than five minutes later, he'd have known he was close even if Lloyd hadn't been yanking on his arm. There were three vehicles alongside the road, none of them his SUV, and all empty. He jammed on the brakes, got the bike stopped and was across the road in seconds.

It was a steep ravine and about fifteen feet down, his SUV was wheels up, resting on its driver's side. Four people, none that he recognized, were standing near the vehicle. One woman was squatting and it looked as if she was trying to talk to Raney.

Who was still inside. Slumped over the steering wheel.

Please let her be alive. Please. Please.

He half slid down the rocky, weed-covered slope. He heard sirens coming closer but he wasn't waiting. He squatted next to the woman and knocked gently on the window. "Raney," he said.

"She's unconscious," said the woman.

"Raney, sweetheart," he said.

She opened her eyes, turned her head and gave him a weak smile.

"I guess she was just waiting for you," the woman said, awe in her voice.

Chase ignored the comment. He looked Raney in the eye. "Hang on," he said. "Just hang on. Help is coming. We're going to get this back on its wheels and get you out of there."

Her eyelids fluttered shut.

Chase pounded his hand on the frame of the SUV. "Stay with me, Raney. Stay with me."

He turned and saw four men in matching coats. Volunteer firefighters. He recognized one of them. Hank Beaumont had been their senior class president. He was pretty sure the man knew him, too, but fortunately, he wasn't interested in chatting it up. He was all business, his eyes focused on Raney.

"One person in the vehicle?"

"Yes," Chase said.

"Do we know the extent of her injuries?"

"No. Listen, we need to get this vehicle righted and get her out of there."

"Step back," Hank ordered.

Chase didn't move. "I'm a cop. St. Louis PD."

The man's eyes softened. "I know. I heard you were back in town, Chase. That was my mother-in-law who was behind you checking out at the grocery store. I'm guessing this is your wife, and I'm sorry about that, but it also means that you're not acting in any official capacity. So stand back and let us do our job."

Chase moved and shoved his hands in his pockets. Lloyd came up and stood next to him. "She's not dead," the man said.

No, she wasn't. But whoever had caused this

accident was a dead man. Chase split his attention—shifting quickly from watching the four firemen right the vehicle to viewing the small crowd that had gathered.

It wasn't all that unusual for a perpetrator to hang around a scene. Whether it was in celebration or defiance that they could be in plain sight, or maybe some crazy need for closure, a good cop always watched the people at the scene. Sophisticated police departments caught it on film.

The Ravesville Police Department was neither sophisticated nor timely since they had yet to arrive.

But the SUV was upright and they were opening the driver's door. Hank had his head inside, talking to Raney.

Chase had waited long enough. He skirted around the small group and approached from the passenger side. Before anyone could stop him, he opened the door and slipped inside.

"Hey," he said softly.

She was still wearing her seat belt. It was pulled tight and he suspected she'd have some bruising. The air bag had inflated, then deflated, leaving a thick residue behind. It was on her shirt, her cheeks, her nose. He could see a red mark on her forehead, near the hairline on the left side. The skin had not broken but it looked as if she had a lump.

"Mrs. Hollister," Hank said, still at the door. "I'm going to put a neck collar around you, just as a precaution."

"Okay," Raney said. "But I didn't hurt my neck."

"You hit your head," Chase said, working hard to keep his tone neutral. He didn't want to scare her.

She lifted her fingers to her forehead. "I did?"

Hank reached in and fastened a cervical collar around Raney. It made her look even more delicate, and Chase fought down the anger that was threatening to cloud his ability to think. Focus. He needed to focus.

The firemen transferred her from the SUV to a gurney and an EMT took her vitals. Chase stood close enough that he could hear. Blood pressure, 123 over 77. That was fine. Pulse, 79. Maybe a little fast but that was to be expected. The EMT checked her eyes, her reflexes, asked about pain. Raney asked to sit up and the EMT agreed. Chase let out a breath.

Chase finally heard the sounds of an approaching siren and figured it had to be the responding officer. When the car came into view, it slowed quickly and pulled up close, blocking the road. The door opened and Gary Blake, Summer's ex, got out.

He walked up to Hank Beaumont, and Chase didn't see what he'd expected. Cops and firefighters were kindred spirits, especially in a small community. They showed up at all the same events, shared bad jokes and a general dislike for administration. But between Beaumont and Blake there was no friendly recognition, no casual camaraderie. The exchange seemed more forced, as if both men knew they had to do it and just wanted to get it over with as quickly as possible.

If Raney had a head injury, this had the potential to end badly for a number of reasons. Was she seconds away from blurting out that she was Lorraine Taylor and what had brought her to Ravesville? He hated to put pressure on her but the stakes were too high. "Remember," Chase whispered, barely moving his lips. "You're Raney Hollister."

"I know," she said, her tone almost sounding amused. "I'm not—"

Blake turned away from the fire chief and stepped toward Raney. He looked bored. "You were the driver," he said when he got in front of Raney.

Chase couldn't tell if it was a statement or a question.

"I need to see your license," Blake said.

It pissed Chase off that the man hadn't even bothered to inquire whether Raney was okay. But Chase kept his thoughts to himself. He and Raney were trying to stay under the radar. Mixing it up with the local police would only hurt those efforts.

Chase had pulled Raney's purse from the vehicle and now he handed it to her. Raney unzipped it and pulled out her billfold. Without hesitation she handed over her license, the Lorraine Hollister one she'd been given shortly after the wedding ceremony. Chase sent a silent prayer upward. At the time, he'd thought it was unnecessary to go to such extremes. He'd been irritated about waiting around for it. But now it might be what got them out of this.

Blake took it without comment and looked at it quickly. He copied down the number onto the report he was making. He handed it back to Raney. Then he shifted his attention to Chase and narrowed his eyes. "You're that Hollister kid that everybody's been talking about."

That good-for-nothing, troublemaking Hollister kid. The man's tone said it all.

Chase rubbed his forehead where a raging headache that had started when he'd seen Lloyd's motorcycle flying down the road and intensified when he'd seen Raney with a cervical collar around her neck was simmering behind his right eyeball. He'd be ninety and the good people of Ravesville would still be talking about him.

"I've heard about your brother Bray," Gary Blake said.

"I imagine you have," Chase said.

"I'd have been better off if I'd have let him marry Summer Wright."

Neither Chase nor Raney responded. Blake didn't seem to notice.

"What happened here?" he asked.

"A car attempted to pass me. They got a little close and I moved over. My tires caught the edge of the road and my car rolled."

"How fast were you going?"

"The speed limit," she answered.

"Of course," Blake said, as if he couldn't care less. As if he'd formed an opinion and that was that. Raney had been either going too fast and paid the consequences or she was a hell of a poor driver.

Chase doubted it was either. She was simply not used to these roads and the driver had unfortunately picked the narrowest portion of the road to pass.

"Where's the other vehicle?" Blake asked.

Raney licked her lips. "I don't think it stopped. Perhaps they didn't see me lose control."

Now Blake looked at her. "That seems unlikely, doesn't it?" he asked.

"It certainly wasn't helpful," Raney said, not answering the question.

Blake looked at his watch. "Can you describe the other vehicle?"

"Black or dark blue. Some kind of SUV."

It was subtle but Gary Blake's jaw muscle jerked just a little. Most people wouldn't have seen it but Chase was a master interrogator. He always watched for the *tell*, the movement, the gesture, the nervous habit that said somebody was lying or just about to lie.

When Blake didn't offer anything up, Chase pushed. "Ring any bells?"

Blake looked bored. "There are a whole lot of black or blue SUVs that go through Ravesville on a given day."

He supposed that was true.

"Did you see the driver?" Blake asked. He'd put his pen down.

"The driver was wearing some kind of hooded sweatshirt and sunglasses. Had some scraggily facial hair."

Same small jerk of the jaw. Then Blake ran his pen down the paper. He looked up at Raney. "The fire chief said you bumped your head. Are you going to seek medical treatment?"

"No. I'm fine."

As far as Chase was concerned, the jury was still out on that one. Raney was doing well with Blake, not fumbling for answers. But head injuries were tricky. People had walked away from accidents fine and hours later, had blood clots and dropped dead.

Blake was only asking because he had to check a box on his report. He did that and then put his pen back in his pocket.

Chase couldn't decide if he was relieved that the incident wasn't going to blow their cover out of the water or really, truly pissed that Blake was such a lazy cop. He was acting as if they, as outsiders, were barely worth his time to fill out a report. Nobody was dead. He was still going to get to go home early.

Blake might not be interested in the other driver but Chase was. He intended to find him. His irresponsibility could have killed Raney.

Blake looked at Chase. "Planning on staying long in Ravesville?"

"Just long enough for me to get my mother's house ready to sell," he said.

"Brick Doogan was a son of a bitch."

He and Gary Blake were not going to bond over their common dislike. "Well, he's dead now."

Blake laughed, a deep bark of a sound. "Got that right," he said. He took a couple steps before turning back. "You two have a good day," he said. "I suggest you try going less than the speed limit, Mrs. Hollister."

"GOOD JOB," CHASE MURMURED, as they watched Gary Blake walk away.

She'd just lied to a police officer. Deliberately withheld the truth. "Thank you," she said. She wasn't ready to say anything more.

"I know you told the paramedic that you didn't want to go to the hospital. I want you to reconsider."

She shook her head. "I'm okay. Really."

He didn't look happy. Well, he was likely to be significantly unhappier when he learned the truth. But she didn't intend to tell him here. She would do it at the house, where they could talk without being overheard.

She watched as the tow truck pulled away. It had Chase's SUV, which had a big dent in the passenger-side fender and a flat rear tire on that same side, and was taking it into Ravesville. Hank Beaumont came up and stood before them. "You two need a ride home?"

"Thank you," Chase said. He helped Raney into the backseat of the red SUV. It was a short drive home.

"Pleasure to meet you, Raney," Hank said. "Good luck with the recovery."

They were barely inside the house when Chase got on the telephone. She could only hear his side of the conversation but gathered enough to know that he was talking to someone about getting another vehicle. She closed her eyes, rested her head on the pillow and tuned the rest of the conversation out. When the call ended, he came into the living room.

She was lying on the couch, and he took the chair opposite of her. "Can I get you anything?" he asked.

She shook her head. "Isn't it going to look odd when we suddenly have a different vehicle here?"

He nodded. "We have to take that chance. It's better than not having wheels if we need to get out of here in a hurry. They're going to lay a paper trail so that the vehicle looks as if it belonged to Raney Smith who recently became Raney Hollister."

It was truly frightening how quickly resources could be marshaled to make something look different than it was. It made her wonder if anything in life was real.

And she had done her part to add to the deception. It was time for Chase to know the truth.

But before she could open her mouth, he

asked, "Do you think you're up to going through it one more time?"

"Why?"

"Humor me," he said. "I'm going to find that other driver and make sure he understands what happened here."

Yeah, well, that might not be such a good idea. "Uh... Chase, the accident didn't happen exactly like I told Gary Blake."

Chapter Nine

There was a short pause, a very short one, before Chase said, "Okay."

He was probably a very good detective. She knew that she'd surprised him but he was controlling his response.

"How about we start at the beginning?" he said.

She stared at her hands, her fingers. It was funny how these things worked. While it had probably lasted less than a few seconds, she had a very vivid memory of seeing her hands wrapped tight around the steering wheel, her fingers tensed, as she saw the right front fender of the other vehicle veer toward her. "I probably should have been more forthcoming when I asked to borrow your vehicle. I do have a driver's license and I do drive, it's just that I don't very often. I don't even own a car. And so while I'm telling you this, I want you to keep that in the back of your mind. It's possible that

I overreacted, that I made a mistake because I'm an inexperienced driver driving in an area that I'm not familiar with."

"Duly noted," he said. "Keep going."

She swallowed hard. "When I left here, I went to the hardware store," she said. "Damn." She looked up. "Your nails are in a sack in the backseat."

He held up a hand. "We'll worry about that later. Go on."

"It was hot and I was thirsty. And, while it may sound silly and sort of self-centered, I wasn't ready to come back yet. It's been a while since I've been able to do what I wanted. After I was moved to the safe house in Miami, my movements were very controlled. I could no longer go to events, or take long walks, or do any of the things that I wanted to do. So today it just felt good to be out on my own, without somebody watching my every move."

"Not self-centered," he said. "Not one bit."

"Anyway, I decided to go to the café to get an iced tea. Summer was working." She did not mention seeing the bruise on the woman's back. First things first. "While I was there, Sheila Stanton came in."

"Did the two of you talk?"

"She asked some questions, wanted to know how we met. I told her through mutual friends.

It was a short conversation. Uncomfortable for me. I don't know how she felt. She's hard to read."

"Then what happened?"

"I left the café. I was coming back to the house. I saw the car behind me. I had my sunglasses on but I'm sure it was black or dark blue, maybe a very dark gray. It was coming up fast behind me and that did make me nervous. I slowed down a little, hoping that it would pass me. And when it did, it swerved toward me. I know I told Gary Blake that it got too close and I overreacted but that's only partially true. It's possible that the vehicle was deliberately trying to push me off the road."

She saw a quick change in his eyes before he shut it down. He'd gone into cop mode. "Tell me about the driver," he said, his voice still calm.

It made her feel sick to relive those few seconds. She held up one hand and put the other on her stomach. "You might want to keep your distance. The tea and pie I had at Wright Here, Wright Now may be making a return appearance."

Instead of stepping back, he moved forward and sat next to her on the couch. He wrapped an arm around her shoulder. "Take your time," he said.

She swallowed hard. "I told Gary Blake the truth about that. The hood was loose around his face, making it hard to see." She ran her hand through her short hair. "There is something that is nagging at me. Making me think that I missed something."

"What do you mean?"

"I can't explain any better than that. In the blink of an eye, I was taking in all these things. The driver turning the steering wheel. The front fender getting close. My tires losing traction. Too much stimuli. I'm worried that I may not have processed it right."

"You did fine. You're doing fine," he added.

She shook her head. "I should have let him hit me. That would have at least slowed him down. Maybe his vehicle would have been tangled up with mine."

"And you might have been hurt badly," he said. "You did the right thing. You tried to avoid the danger. If it was deliberate, I suspect he picked that spot carefully, because that's where the road is narrow and the drop-off steep."

She'd been thinking the same thing while she'd sat alongside the road, waiting for the Ravesville police to show up. But to hear him say it, to know that the action may have been so cold-blooded, made her blood turn to ice.

"Why didn't you tell Gary Blake the truth?"

She looked him in the eye. "When I first met Harry Malone, there was something about him that made me uneasy. I couldn't put my finger on it. He was pleasant, good with the clients and the rest of the staff at Next Steps thought he was wonderful. So I discounted my concerns. And look where that got me."

He didn't say anything but she could tell he was listening intently.

"In the dark, alone, a person has a lot of time to think. To make bargains. Promises. One of mine was to trust my instincts more. And my instincts tell me that Gary Blake isn't a good guy. I thought if I told him the truth, then our whole story might unravel and I didn't want to take that chance."

He smiled. "You've made me feel better."

"Why?"

"Because if you were thinking that clearly, I don't think that bump on your head can be all that bad. I'm going to give up trying to convince you to seek medical treatment."

She pulled away. "That's it? That's all you can say?"

He shook his head. "Of course not. But you need to know that I think you made the right decision. Blake may not be a dirty cop but he's a lazy one, and that's enough for me not to trust him, either."

"Do you think it's the people who tried to kill me before?" she asked, proud that she was keeping her voice mostly steady. "Have they found me?"

He tightened his strong arm around her shoulders and pulled her close. "I don't know," he said honestly. "If it was, I'm surprised that the driver didn't stick around to make sure he'd gotten the job done. But maybe others stopped so quickly that he got scared and got the hell out of there. But none of that matters because he isn't going to get another chance. I can guarantee you that."

"But if it is, then somebody knows that Raney Hollister is the old Lorraine Taylor. They can find out where we live. Come here."

"And if they do, I will handle it," he said calmly. "I will not let anyone hurt you. You have to believe me."

She suddenly felt very warm and she was very aware that they were alone in the house, unlikely to have any visitors anytime soon.

He was so close, his arm still wrapped around her shoulder. She turned her face. His lips were right there.

She should look away, get up, do something. But she stayed perfectly still. Waiting.

It was so still that she could hear the ticking of the kitchen clock, a whole room away. He took a breath. A deep one, making his broad chest expand.

"Chase," she said.

He let the breath out and carefully pulled his arm away. Her shoulder felt bare. Cold.

He got up. "Try to get a little rest. I won't let you sleep for long," he said. "Just as a precaution against a concussion."

Dr. Chase Hollister reporting for duty. "Chase," she said again.

He shook his head sharply. "I'll be outside."

CHASE DIDN'T HAVE any damn nails to hammer so he cranked up the chain saw and started attacking some trees. The wind had picked up and branches were whipping around, making the effort even more of a challenge. He held the chain saw above his head, slicing and dicing the unsuspecting limbs, and moving fast when they tumbled to the ground.

He was in trouble. He was getting sucked in by the unique combination that was all Raney. Trust and innocence along with a bold invitation to play.

When he'd talked to Dawson on the telephone about getting another vehicle, his partner had asked him how the assignment was going. Fine. That was what he'd said. He certainly couldn't tell his partner that he was a punch away from going down for the count.

He wanted her. In his bed. Under him, on top, hell, it didn't matter. As long as it happened. Lust was a dangerous thing. It had started small, probably about the time he'd seen her standing in the wedding dress, her sexy blond hair tousled from struggling with the gown, her breasts almost spilling out over the strapless top. It had spiked when he'd opened the door that first morning and seen her sprawled across the bed, her shorts short and her top riding up.

He'd managed to claw it back, to keep it at bay, until he'd seen Keith getting cozy with her at the dining room table. And now, after coming this close to losing her, his control was frayed.

She was injured. That should have been enough to cool his jets. But it didn't. Which was a big problem for her. If she was right, and it had been deliberate, then he needed to keep his head in the game and other parts checked at the door.

He kicked at some of the downed limbs. They might make some decent firewood. He started trimming the smaller branches off, then cutting the bigger limbs into manageable chunks. All the time his mind was racing.

A dark SUV.

Maybe Raney's inexperience had caught up with her and she'd overreacted. But that did not explain why the driver didn't stop. Unless he was uninsured or running from the law and didn't want to get involved in a police investigation. There were a thousand reasons why people chose not to get involved.

Whiz kid Keith's car had been black, too. Although not an SUV. Anyway, Raney was helping him. There was no reason for him to want to hurt her. Was there?

Was it even possible that it was one of Harry Malone's paid goons? If Malone was behind it, his people weren't going to get a second chance. He intended to stick to Raney like glue. He was going to put his libido on ice and she was never going to know that she had him in knots.

After Raney's confession, he'd sent Dawson a text. He wanted more firepower in the house, in more rooms, so that they couldn't ever be caught off guard.

He looked off to the west. The sky was still clear but the wind was picking up, blowing strong enough to toss the small branches around the yard. He picked up what he could and piled them around the corner of the porch, out of the breeze. His newly cut firewood went into a separate pile, closer to the house.

He wondered if Raney enjoyed a fire on a cold winter day. He had a gas fireplace in his apartment in St. Louis. His sterile little space had always suited him. Up until now.

He'd escaped from this house once. Why the hell was he letting it pull him back?

He threw more wood onto the pile. The house would be sold by winter. Another family would enjoy the fruits of his labor.

He put the chain saw away and locked the garage. When he returned to the house, it was quiet. No radio playing. No clatter of Raney's keyboard. He looked around downstairs.

Then he quietly walked upstairs. Knocked on her door. Waited. When she didn't answer, he didn't hesitate to turn the knob.

She was sleeping. This time on her back. Still sideways—head at ten, toes at four. One arm thrown above her head, the other close to her side. She was still wearing the clothes that she'd had on earlier.

She was beautiful. Even with a nasty bump on her forehead.

He knocked on the wall. She didn't move. Concerned, he approached the bed.

"Raney," he said softly.

No response.

"Raney." Loud this time.

She blinked, once, twice, then opened her eyes wide. She smiled at him. "You do not have to yell. I bumped my head, not my ears."

He wanted to laugh. "I knocked. You didn't wake up. I was worried."

"You told me to rest."

He sat down on the edge of the bed. "How do you feel?"

"I have a little headache. I suppose that's to be expected. My ribs that were already sore took a beating from the seat belt. But I was used to babying them so it will just be more of the same. I suspect I'll be fine by tomorrow."

"Do you want something to eat?"

She considered. "No, I don't think so."

She should eat. "I know how to heat up a mean cup of soup."

She smiled. "I suspect you do. But that can't be what you were expecting when you signed up for guard duty. You probably figured the witness could at least feed herself."

He'd expected to be bored out of his mind. Antsy to get back to the city. Irritated that Lorraine Taylor was keeping him in Ravesville. "I expected to make sure you stayed safe," he said. "Right now, I think that includes fixing dinner."

"Maybe just some tea and toast. I'll come down and get it."

He held up a hand. "Please. If I don't get to turn on the stove, at least let me bring it to you."

She nodded and he stood up. He thought about trying to convince her to eat more. But he knew that she was a grown woman—she could make decisions about what she wanted. If she got hungry in the middle of the night, she could get a snack.

He went down to the kitchen, heated the water and toasted the bread. Then he carried them upstairs. She was sitting up in bed.

He handed her the small plate with the two pieces of toast. He put the tea on the table next to the bed. He was more grateful than ever that Brick had purchased a mattress and box spring in anticipation of Lloyd's return home. Raney's bed was really coming in handy now.

"What are your plans for the night?" she asked, taking small bites.

"I'm going to tape up some of the rooms. I want to get them ready to paint." Maybe he'd even work up the courage to go into Brick's bedroom. He'd take a big garbage sack and just start pitching. While he didn't feel the man in the rest of the house, he suspected that would change when he entered the bedroom.

"I'll be ready to help by tomorrow. For sure," she added.

Just having her in the house helped. But he couldn't admit that. "You better be," he said, winking at her. "There's woodwork that needs stripping."

HE'D PUT BUTTER and peanut butter on her toast, just the way she liked it. Which meant that he'd been watching how she fixed her breakfast.

What the hell did that mean?

More than she could contemplate with a nagging headache. She ate toast and drank half of her tea. Then she pushed herself out of bed, took off her clothes and put on her pajamas. A trip across the hall accomplished all other necessary tasks, including brushing her teeth and washing her face.

On the way back to her bed, she opened her window. The room was warm, warmer than it had been the night before. The wind that rushed in was not significantly cooler, but she left the window open anyway. It would likely cool off later.

She crawled back into bed, tossing her new sheets to the end of it. It was not yet seven o'clock and she was settling in for the night. Like an old lady. All she needed was a cat and a cane.

You rolled off a road today, she reminded herself. *You're entitled to a little TLC.*

It had been the same way when she'd escaped from Harry Malone. She'd craved sleep but the police had been insistent upon talking to her. She could still remember sitting in cold rooms, with brown laminate tables and hard chairs. There were times when she'd simply laid her head down on the table and closed her eyes.

Cup of coffee, Ms. Taylor? Perhaps a sandwich? They'd pretended to be concerned about her needs and her welfare, but what they'd really wanted was her testimony. By the time they'd finished with her, she'd been just about finished, one nerve short of a full-blown meltdown.

She'd gone home and slept for three days.

Tonight, she thought another eight hours would take care of things nicely. Gary Blake certainly hadn't been interested in having a prolonged conversation with her. By the way he'd been looking at his watch, she'd gotten the impression that he had a pressing engagement and didn't want to be late.

On the opposite side of the spectrum, Chase had been wonderful. Since the moment he'd arrived at the scene, he'd been quietly capable. She'd felt bad about his SUV but she could tell that he truly wasn't concerned about the vehicle.

Tomorrow she'd hit the ground running. She closed her eyes.

And didn't open them again until she heard something hit the house. She sprang up in bed, her back hitting the plaster wall. The wind was howling and lightning was splitting the sky.

Heart racing, she reached for the lamp. She caught the shade with the back of her hand and barely managed to keep it upright. She felt for the switch, flipped it, and nothing happened. She flipped it again and again.

Something hit the house again and she saw movement in the corner. She screamed, wrapped her hand around the base of the lamp, jerked hard, felt the cord pull from the wall and cocked her arm.

She would fight until her very last breath.

Chapter Ten

Chase woke up to a woman's screams. He grabbed his gun and was off the couch and halfway up the stairs before he realized that the light in the kitchen that he'd left on was now off. He wasn't surprised. It was storming and the damn electricity was always going out.

He charged ahead, listening for another scream. He had only heard one.

He turned the knob of Raney's room, pushed the door open with his foot and swung through the doorway. The room was absolutely dark. He couldn't see a damn thing.

He heard the roll of thunder. Counted. Got to two before a spear of lightning brightened the sky. Long enough for him to see Raney on the corner of the bed, her knees drawn up to her chest, holding the old lamp in her hand, as if she was going for the shot-put record. Her eyes were huge.

Then the room went dark again.

"Raney?" he said.

She didn't answer. He took a step toward the bed. "Honey, it's okay. Just a little Missouri storm."

Still no answer. He got close enough that he could touch her. For a minute, he thought the damn bed was shaking. Then realized it was her.

He forgot all about keeping his distance. He sat on the bed, gently disengaged the lamp from her fingers, set it back on the nightstand and pulled her into his arms. She was all bare arms and legs, and when he tucked her head into his chest, he caught a whiff of mint from her toothpaste. "There, there," he said. "Nothing to be afraid of." He wrapped both arms around her and gently rocked her.

After a long minute, her shaking subsided. But he didn't let go. Her skin was so soft. She smelled so good.

He moved one hand up to the nape of her neck and ran his fingers through the soft, sexy hair. He heard her breath catch.

Would she tell him to stop?

Not yet, he willed. He needed to hold her.

"What happened?" he whispered.

"I heard something and then I thought I saw something in the corner and I freaked out."

He strained his eyes toward the dark corner. He needed another bolt of lightning. "I don't see..."

"I think it was the curtain. The wind was whipping it around. I...should not have screamed. It reminded me of...before."

"Before what?"

She didn't answer for a long minute. He heard the rumble of thunder and waited for the lightning. At the exact moment it struck, she lifted her head and looked him in the eye. Her eyes were bright, shiny with unshed tears. He gathered her closer as the darkness settled around them again. The wind was really howling now.

"Shortly after Harry Malone abducted me, he left me in this small room. There was no bed, just an old two-drawer metal filing cabinet that was completely empty. I slept on the floor. It was a beat-up old wooden floor. Worse than the floors in this house," she added.

He steeled himself. She was trying to lighten the mood but he had a feeling that whatever was coming, it was going to be hard to hear. Another rubble of thunder shook the house and Raney jerked. He gathered her just a little closer.

"It started to storm while he was gone. It was a horrific storm and the entire time, I kept praying that the wind would blow hard enough that the apartment or the house, whatever I was in, would come apart. And then someone would know I was there. Someone would see me."

"What happened?"

"He came back. Just as the storm seemed to hit its peak. I can still see him flinging open the door so hard that it hit the wall. He was drenched. Tonight I heard something hit the house and then I saw the movement and for a minute, I was back there."

He wanted to kill Harry Malone. "What happened when he came back?"

She sighed. "He was angry about something. I'm not sure what. All I know is that he punched and kicked me, adding to the assortment of bruises, bumps and cracked ribs that I already had."

Unconsciously, he stroked her ribs through her thin shirt. The idea of a man taking his foot and kicking her made him realize that killing Harry Malone would be too nice. He was going to break every one of his ribs first. Maybe his legs, too.

"I'm sorry," he said simply.

"He never...you know."

"I read the report," he said, which was why he knew it was a damn miracle that this was the first flashback that he'd witnessed. She hadn't been raped but she'd been brutalized, kicked like a rabid dog.

"Really," she said, as if she were trying to reassure him, "I was one of the lucky ones. I got away. Those other poor women didn't."

"But you're making sure he pays for his sins. You're getting vindication for each of them."

"You know he took my picture?"

"I did know that," he said, keeping his tone neutral.

"The first time he did that, I didn't know what to think. He'd tossed me into this barren room and was acting like I'd come for a photo shoot. 'Stand up. Sit down. Put your arms above your head.' It was bizarre. He must have taken eight, maybe ten different shots. And with no explanation, he left. It was crazy, just crazy."

The storm was hitting its peak in intensity. Lightning cracked, briefly brightening the room. "Rain is really coming down hard now," he said, wanting to give her a chance to change the subject.

She didn't take the bait. "The next time he came back, he showed me pictures of the other women. I still didn't get it at first. Because the women looked okay. Scared, sure. But not hurt. In a crazy way, I was hopeful that maybe I wasn't all alone. That maybe the other women were down the hall. But he kept making me look at more pictures on his camera. And the women started looking worse. Bruised. Dirty. So tired. I started to get it. And then I saw the pictures where they were dead." Her voice had cracked at the end.

"All part of his psychological torture," he said.

"Yeah. He wanted me to know what my fate was going to be. It was so horrible to know that these women had been alive and then killed, and to know that the same thing was going to happen to me."

"He was pretty sure of himself," Chase said. The son of a bitch had underestimated Raney. He'd only shown her the pictures because he was so confident that she'd never get away.

"He told me that he was a storyteller. That the women in the pictures were characters in his story and that he liked me so much that he wanted me to have my own story. It became very clear that he got off on showing me what had happened to the others."

He could hear the anguish in her voice. He bent his head, brushed a kiss across her shoulder. "It's over, Raney."

She sucked in a deep breath. "All I knew is that if I didn't find a way to get away from him, it wouldn't be long before another victim was looking at pictures of me."

He put his hand under her chin and gently turned her face. If there had been light, he would have been able to look her in the eye. "But he underestimated you," he said. "You were smarter and braver than he could have ever anticipated. You got away when he was absolutely confident that you couldn't."

"Never underestimate the power of nail polish," she said, her tone solemn.

When he'd read the report, he'd been both fascinated and impressed. He wanted to hear her explanation but didn't want her to have to relive it if it was painful. "You didn't, that's what is important."

"It was all I had. When Malone grabbed me as I was walking home from Next Steps, he took my purse and my cell phone. I never saw them again. But he didn't think to check my pockets. And I had a bottle of topcoat. I'd polished my nails at home that morning but had been running late and decided I'd add the topcoat—that's the final coat that makes the nails shiny—during my dinner break. I did that and dropped it in my skirt pocket."

"And you figured out how to use that as a weapon."

"Not at first. There was nothing in the room

but that damn empty filing cabinet. I tried to pick it up, thinking maybe I could throw it at him, but there was no way. I stared at it for hours until I finally figured out that it was put together with bolts and screws. And I could use the washers, the flat metal part that secures the screw."

"But you didn't have any tools."

"No. Not even a darn plastic knife. Malone wasn't stupid. I had to use my fingers. At one point, I was totally freaked out because I sliced my finger up and it was bleeding and there was blood on the screws that I couldn't get off. I was so afraid that he was somehow going to see that. And there was no way that I could get some of the screws loose to get to those particular washers. But I finally managed to get six. Then I used the topcoat to bind them together, so that they made a hard round stack. Each washer was thin and so six together didn't make much but I thought it might be enough."

"For?" he asked.

"To mess up the lock. Before he came into the room, I could hear him walk down the squeaky hallway and then flip the bolt lock on the outside of the door. When he left, same routine in reverse. My plan was to stuff my contraption into the bolt-lock hole so that when he turned the lock to throw the cylinder, the cylinder would get jammed and the lock wouldn't catch."

"Smart."

"I don't know about that. But it was the only plan I had and time was running out. He would occasionally give me some water but no food. That's what he used the filing cabinet for. He would set my water on it. Isn't that crazy? He didn't care about killing me but he didn't want to set my water on the floor?"

"The mind can be very twisted," he said.

"All I knew is that I was getting very weak, and based on the pictures that I'd seen of those other women, I thought my time was running out. My plan was full of holes. I needed to smear a fresh layer of topcoat on one end of my washers just at the right time so that when I inserted them into the hole, the polish would adhere to the back of the lock receptacle. Assuming I managed that, my washers needed to be thick enough to keep the door from locking. So many unknowns, not the least of which was that I needed to get near the door without him seeing me."

"But you knew you had to do it."

"Yes. And it helped that he was a man of patterns. I knew he would come in, set the water down on the filing cabinet and then start posing me for pictures. He always kept

the door open when he was with me, which
told me that there was no one else around. I'm
sure he assumed that if I tried to escape that
it would be relatively easy to overpower me.
Anyway, he had a favorite pose. I would have
to stand up, put both hands around my neck
and tilt my head just so, to make it look as if I
was strangling myself."

Malone was a sick bastard.

"So I did it. Just like I had before. But then
I pretended that I'd somehow choked myself. I
started gagging and coughing and I was doing
such a job of it, I actually thought I was going
to throw up. I knew that Malone was a germ
freak. At Next Steps, he would sanitize the
workstation before he would use the computer
or the telephone. He wouldn't eat food that
somebody had left in the break room because
he hadn't seen it get prepared. I was counting on the fact that it was going to gross him
out and he'd move away. It did and he turned
away. Long enough for me to shove the washers in the hole."

"What happened when he left?"

"I was shaking so hard I could barely move.
I heard him flip the lock like always. It didn't
catch. He opened the door, flipping the lock
back and forth. The cylinder was working fine,
of course. Then he looked into the hole. When

you look into a dark hole, you can't see anything. He poked his finger in and maybe felt
something, maybe didn't, but he just looked
irritated, not suspicious of me. He closed the
door. I heard his footsteps. I figured he was
going in search of a flashlight or something. I
didn't wait around to find out. I got out of that
room fast. Made it to the street. Didn't know
where I was but knew it was a poor urban area.
It was nighttime. I just started running as fast
as I could. I turned a corner and flagged down
a car. I'm surprised they stopped because I was
a mess. But they did. And the rest is history."

"Amazing," Chase said.

"He would have realized very quickly that
I was gone. Maybe he tried to come after me
and catch me. Maybe he simply decided to
cut his losses and run. The police caught him
in his car. They think that he was on the way
to a small private airstrip. He has his own
plane and perhaps was contemplating leaving
the country. Of course, he denied everything.
And he'd been smart. Besides kicking me, he'd
never physically touched me. There was none
of my DNA on him, just at the apartment."

But the jury would believe her. They would
hear from her, from the old couple who picked
her up on the road, from the detectives who
had taken her original statement. They would

hear from the forensics experts who could place her in that apartment because of the blood she'd left behind in the filing cabinet.

Lightning flashed and he hoped to see peace in her eyes. But he saw something else, something more.

Heat. Want.

"Chase," she said, her voice a mere whisper. "Stay with me."

He knew all the reasons why it was a bad idea. But none of that mattered. What did was that Raney, sweet Raney with her soft skin and sexy hair, was in his arms.

He leaned in, found her mouth and kissed her. Her mouth was warm and wet and when he settled in, it seemed as if he'd been waiting a lifetime for kisses like this.

He framed her face, running the pads of his thumbs across her cheeks, her little ears, her long, pretty neck. The kisses were long and succulent and he felt as though he could jump tall buildings.

The storm outside was moving away, leaving only the occasional quiet rumble of thunder in the distance. "Raney?" he whispered, giving her one last chance.

In answer, she put his hand on her breast.

He made love to her. And when she came apart in his arms, and he quickly followed her over the edge, he felt something shift in his soul, and knew that nothing would ever again be the same.

RANEY DOZED AND when she woke up, the room was dark and she was very warm. It dawned on her that Chase Hollister made one hell of a blanket.

He was naked and wrapped around her.

Delicious. The sex had been better than red-velvet cake with cream-cheese frosting. And that was saying something in her world. He'd been intensely focused on learning her body, understanding her needs, pleasuring her.

That could easily go to a girl's head.

She stretched a leg and he pulled her in just a little tighter. "Doing okay?" he asked, his voice husky with sleep. "Does this hurt your ribs?"

"No, it's fine," she said. "It doesn't sound as if it's raining anymore."

"Uh-huh," he said.

Would he roll over, roll away, now that she no longer needed his comfort? Sex with her husband had been like that. They'd do it and he'd no more than finish up before he'd flop on his back with his hands folded on his chest and be snoring in five minutes. Oblivious to her needs.

She waited. Counted to one hundred. Did it twice more. "Chase?" she said.

"Yes?"

"I… I don't want you to think that you have to keep holding me. I'm really okay."

He sighed. "So you're chatty after sex?"

Was she? "Uh… I don't think so."

"Good. Talking takes energy and I'm trying to conserve mine." He flexed his hips and she could feel him pressing into her. He appeared to be recovering just fine.

"For?" she asked, letting blonde Raney have full reign.

He neatly flipped her on her back. Still on his side, he bent his head to her breast and took a nipple into his mouth. Heat arced through her core and a soft moan escaped.

He lifted his mouth, barely breaking contact. "For this."

Heat. Need. Blind want. It raced through her. She moved quickly, bringing a hand up, placing it flat on his chest, pushing hard. He went with it, falling onto his back.

This man wasn't oblivious. He was terribly sexy and wonderfully aroused. She straddled him. "I'm ready. But this time I get to drive."

Chapter Eleven

The next time Raney woke up, the room was flooded with light. Natural light. It was morning. She wondered if the electricity had come back on. The cord of the lamp lay on the floor, disconnected from the outlet.

Chase was still wrapped around her. His knees tucked behind her knees. His arm casually draped across her stomach. His chin resting on her head.

Perfect.

"Good morning," he whispered.

She wondered how long he'd been awake. She hoped she hadn't snored. "Hi," she said. "What time is it?"

"I'd say about seven. Ready for coffee?"

"Of course. 24/7."

He laughed. "My kind of girl."

Was she Chase Hollister's girl? Lover, sure. But girl? That somehow seemed more intimate, more special. She didn't have a great deal of experience with "the morning after." She'd dated one man after her divorce and they'd slept together but never spent the night together. It had been at his apartment and she'd always gotten up and left.

He moved, sitting up in bed. Blonde Raney shifted onto her back so that she could see him. He'd been pretty damn magnificent in the dark. And he was even more so in the light of day. He had his back to her. His sleek shoulders were broad and his back was all firm with muscle that narrowed down nicely to his waist.

She raised up on an elbow, wanting to get a better look. He shifted suddenly, as if just realizing that he was naked. But before he could pull up the sheet, she saw his leg. Saw the fresh scar.

"What happened?" she whispered.

He put his hand over the injury. "Pretty ugly, I know."

"Tell me," she said.

"About six weeks ago, I took a bullet in the thigh. Got lucky in that it didn't break a bone but I had a whole lot of muscle damage."

"Did you have surgery?"

"Right away. I was bleeding badly."

"And you've been crawling up and down off the roof," she said. *And doing other gymnastics in bed*, she silently added, feeling guilty.

"It's fine. The activity strengthens it."

"Why didn't you say anything?" she asked.

She was prepared for him to tell her that it wasn't any of her business. Instead, he looked her in the eye and said, "I didn't want you to be worried that I wasn't a hundred percent capable."

If she had been, that misbelief would have been well and truly debunked at this point. "I think you're one of the most capable people I know," she said.

"I don't want things to be awkward between us," he said, his voice giving no clue as to how he was feeling.

Awkward as in he was concerned that she might not ever let him leave the bed again?

Awkward as in she might be willing to pay for another night like the previous one?

Or awkward in that she might think that last night had meant something to him?

"It won't be awkward." Blonde Raney was such a liar.

"You're sure?"

"Absolutely," she said, swallowing hard.

"I'll get that coffee, then," he said. "Want some toast, too?"

She nodded. Anything that would keep him out of the room longer. She needed to get control.

She supposed what had happened last night had been inevitable. There had been a strong physical attraction between her and Chase since the moment they'd met. They weren't naive teenagers caught up in the moment. They were adults, responding to stimuli, acting in response and fully capable of taking responsibility for their own actions.

It sounded like a dull biology experiment when in reality it had been stunningly beautiful and absolutely exhilarating.

But he didn't want awkward.

She could give him that.

When he came back, he was carrying two steaming cups of coffee in one hand and a plate of toast in the other. He had pulled on a pair of gym shorts.

She reached for the cup, took too fast a sip and burned her tongue.

"Careful," he said.

Somebody should have told her that last night. Before she'd jumped his bones.

He got back into bed and set the plate of toast between them.

She chewed, swallowed and drank her coffee. He did the same. When he was finished, he set down his cup on the nightstand.

He gave her a long look, as if waiting for her questions to commence.

She smiled at him. "You better get started outside."

IT WAS JUST before lunch that he saw two vehicles coming down the road. Both SUVs, similar to what he'd been driving the day before. He put down the scraper that he'd been using to peel the old paint off the porch.

He'd switched jobs this morning after taking a quick peek at the roof to assess the damage done by the storm. Fortunately, it was minimal. Yesterday he'd finished removing all the old shingles and had tacked down the paper. Right before Raney had called him to dinner, thinking it felt like rain, he'd quickly finished covering the work with plastic that Gordy's son-in-law had thoughtfully provided.

He probably could have laid shingles this morning but oddly enough, he hadn't felt all that centered, hadn't felt as if he wanted to be thirty feet in the air.

Raney Taylor had rocked his world, to coin an overused phrase. She'd been warm and wet and when she'd straddled him the second time and said she wanted to drive, he'd thought, *You can take me anywhere. Anytime. Just don't get up*.

In the dark, with her body snuggled up against him, he'd been able to push the second thoughts away. Then this morning, when she'd seen his scar, he'd been truly afraid for just a brief moment that she was going to be repulsed or maybe even scared to be with someone touched by violence when her own life had been torn apart by the same.

But she'd recovered quickly, leaving him to fumble for the right thing to say. He'd settled for *I hope this won't make things awkward* when what he should have said was *I think I'm in over my head.*

So he'd escaped outside. But hadn't gone far. Just in case she happened to stick her head out the door wanting to talk. But she hadn't done that. And now he was going to have to face his partner and the chief of police and pretend as though nothing had happened.

He wiped the sweat out of his eyes and kept his stance relaxed. He had his gun in a holster, safely hidden from view by his long shirt. When the first SUV pulled into the lane and he saw that Dawson was driving, he relaxed for real. His partner got out, looked around and stood with his hands on his hips. "According to my GPS, this road doesn't exist."

Chase smiled. "So how did you find me?"

"Called your cell phone. Which you didn't answer. So I stopped at the café on the corner. A gorgeous redhead with hair to her waist gave me good directions. How's Raney?"

"She's…she's good." Chase had never been the type to kiss and tell and right now would be a hell of a bad time to start. The door of the second vehicle opened. It was the chief.

Under normal circumstances, the man would never have made a two-hour trip to deliver a car. But there was nothing normal about this situation. Raney's testimony was critically important. To the case. To the chief.

Chase shook the man's hand. "Thanks for the vehicle," he said.

"No problem," the chief said. "We won't stay long but I'd like to talk to Raney about the incident yesterday."

Chase almost said no, that he didn't want Raney to have to go through it again. "She's inside," he said. He wasn't sure what she was doing. Maybe she'd gone back to bed. They hadn't gotten all that much sleep the night before.

He held the door open for Dawson and Chief Bates. "Raney," he yelled as he pulled the door shut.

She came from the kitchen. She had on the same tight blue jeans as yesterday, this time with a white T-shirt. "Yes." She stopped short when she saw Dawson and the chief.

"Hello," she said.

"Hi, Raney" from Dawson.

"I was sorry to hear about your trouble yesterday, Ms. Taylor." This from the chief.

Raney nodded. "I'm sorry about the SUV and that you had to make a special trip here."

The chief waved his hand. "Can you tell me what happened?"

She didn't look surprised. She'd heard Chase give Dawson the shorthand version yesterday on the phone. Probably knew that he'd no doubt related that to the chief, but that wasn't going to be good enough. "Of course."

She told her story. The going to town, stopping for a drink at the café, leaving, driving, seeing the vehicle behind her.

The chief interrupted. "When did you notice the car?" he asked sharply.

Raney swallowed. "Not long before it tried to pass me."

The man nodded. "Go on."

"I saw it pull out and I assumed it was going to pass. When it got even with my SUV, it swerved in my direction. I believe it's possible that it was a deliberate attempt to run me off the road. Unfortunately, I didn't realize the shoulder was soft and narrow. My instinct was to avoid getting hit."

"So you saw the driver?" the chief barked.

Chase moved and stood behind Raney's chair. He saw Dawson's eyes widen but he ignored it. Bates might be the chief but he wasn't going to bully Raney.

"I did see the driver. But not in a helpful way," she said, her voice still even.

If the chief was getting to her, she wasn't showing it. She pushed her chair back, refilled her water, taking her time. She was going to make a terrific witness.

She sat back down. "I saw hands. I caught a glimpse of the driver's face and some facial hair but he was wearing a hood, maybe a hooded sweatshirt. It was all so fast. Once I felt my front tire go off the road, I knew I was in trouble and I was concentrating on that."

"You think it was deliberate?" the chief asked, drumming his index finger on the table.

"It seemed to me that he didn't just turn the wheel, he cranked it. And he surely had to know that I ran off the road, but he didn't stop."

The chief didn't say anything for a long minute. Finally, he stood. "Well, again, I'm glad you're okay. Let's head back, Detective," he said, looking at Dawson. He switched his gaze to Chase and inclined his head toward the door.

Chase got the message. The chief wanted to talk to him outside.

They were almost at the vehicles when the chief spoke. "I'm damn concerned about this," he said.

Chase waited.

"What do you think, Detective Hollister?"

"I think Raney got lucky, that we all did. But we don't have any reason to believe that Harry Malone knows that she's here, right?"

Both Dawson and the chief nodded.

"Then, I don't think we should go crazy. The police here aren't going to be helpful and I can't push the issue without raising a whole lot of suspicion. I think we need to be satisfied that our initial plan was a good one and go forward. I won't let Raney out of my sight. She won't go anywhere by herself and I won't leave her alone here."

The chief nodded. "I think you're right," he said. He shook his head. "I sure as hell hope you're right," he added. He took a step toward the car, then stopped. "Do you mind if I use your bathroom before we leave?"

Was the man intending to go back inside and badger Raney? But he couldn't say no. "Up the stairs. Second door on the right."

He started to follow the man inside when Dawson grabbed his arm, hard enough to swing him around. "What the hell?" Chase asked, shaking him off.

"Yeah, what the hell as in what the hell is going on here?" Dawson asked.

Chase said nothing. The silence dragged on.

"Oh, man. I knew it," Dawson said finally. "She is our *witness*."

Chase grit his teeth and tried to remember that Dawson was his very best friend. "I know what she is. And I know what I'm doing."

"Let me stay here with her," Dawson said. "I'll provide the protection."

"Don't be ridiculous. Isn't your wife about to have a baby?"

Dawson nodded. "But I'm worried about you. This is a woman who's been through a lot. Maybe not seeing things clearly. Maybe using…"

The door of the house slammed and the chief walked toward them.

"You," he finished under his breath.

By the time the chief reached them, Dawson had opened the trunk and was unloading the guns that Chase had requested. Rifles and handguns and all kinds of extra bullets. The three men carried everything up onto the porch.

They walked back to the SUV and the chief got behind the wheel. "Check in regularly," he said.

Chase nodded. He made eye contact with Dawson. Gave him another nod. Then he watched the vehicle drive down the lane, make the turn onto the road and finally disappear from sight.

He would protect Raney. He would not lose sight of that.

RANEY STOOD AT the window and watched Chase say goodbye to Detective Roy and Chief Bates. It was not even noon and already she was thinking about a nap.

This morning, she'd stayed in bed for a full half hour after Chase ran out. She had rolled over and, like a crazy woman, sniffed the sheets. She could smell him. Smell them.

The sex had been amazing. Beyond that.

It hadn't been blonde Raney or brunette Raney in his arms. It had just been Raney. She'd lost the ability to plot or plan a response. It had just happened.

And happened again.

Holy moly.

And then he'd brought her coffee, which made him a bit of a prince. And then it had gotten awkward, just exactly what he'd said he'd hoped they could avoid.

When she'd finally gotten out of bed and showered, she'd gone downstairs and heard him on the porch. She'd peeked out the living room window but hadn't had the courage to open the door.

She wanted him to know that she didn't have any expectations that it was going to happen again. That she wasn't waiting for a marriage proposal. That she understood they were in unusual circumstances and that no precedent had been set.

She wanted him to know that he was off the hook.

She wanted him to know that it had been pretty damn terrific.

When she'd heard him yelling her name, she'd hurried from the back, thinking, *Great, he's ready to talk.* She had been surprised to see his partner and the chief of police. She hadn't heard the vehicles pull in. The chief had been a little intense but she supposed that was a job-related characteristic. On the other end of the spectrum was Gary Blake, who acted as though he couldn't care less.

If she had to choose, she'd take intensity any day. And having Chase there had made a difference. When he'd stood behind her, strength had radiated from his core and she'd suddenly felt as if there wasn't anything the chief could throw her way that was going to knock her off her stride.

Too bad she couldn't put Chase Hollister in her pocket when she was on the witness stand. She was going to be all on her own.

The only time she'd been a little nervous was when the chief had walked out with Chase and his partner, clearly interested in having a conversation that didn't include her. She knew they were discussing their plan and whether her staying in Ravesville was still a good idea.

When she'd heard the chief come back inside, she'd prepared herself for bad news. It was hard to believe that just days ago, she'd been complaining to Officer Vincenze about coming here, and now she couldn't quite imagine leaving.

The house needed them. She could feel it.

She'd relaxed when she'd realized that the man was simply using the bathroom. She was staying.

She heard the front door and turned. Chase walked in. "Doing okay?" he asked.

She nodded. "I like your partner. He's got a quiet competence about him."

It was Chase's turn to nod. "He's worried about me."

That surprised her. "Why?"

"Because he sensed the dynamic has changed between the two of us."

Well, she suspected that wasn't exactly what Detective Roy had said. At Next Steps, she frequently overheard young men talk to other young men about their women. Granted, Chase and his partner were older and the vocabulary might have improved but he didn't have to draw her a picture.

"I'm sorry," she said simply.

He shook his head sharply. "I am not sorry. Let's be clear on that."

She felt her insides melt. "We were both consenting adults," she offered.

"You were in a vulnerable position," he said, trying to give her a reason.

She thought about what blonde Raney would say and realized it was exactly what brunette Raney would have. She and Mike hadn't had an honest relationship. She was never going to do that again, regardless of what color her hair was. "I wanted you," she said.

She saw the muscle in his jaw jerk. "Wanted. As in past tense?"

She looked him in the eye. "Want. As in present tense."

He grabbed her hand and pulled her toward the stairs. "Like I told you, I'm a literate man. I understand the difference."

Chapter Twelve

They spent the afternoon making love and dozing. It was less frenzied than the night before and when she let him drive, he felt as if he had a chance of keeping things under control. When she took over the wheel and took him in her mouth, he thought his head was going to pop off his neck.

"I like it when you hold me like this," she said.

He was spooned around her, keeping her tucked close. "Self-preservation," he said. "Left to your own devices, you take up the whole bed."

"I do not," she protested.

"Yes, you do," he said drily. "Head at ten o'clock, feet at four. This way I keep you at twelve and six and we're all much happier."

She was quiet for a long time. He thought maybe she'd fallen back to sleep. But then she shifted. "I need you to know. I am happier than

I have been in a long time. Even though, as recently as yesterday, someone may have deliberately tried to harm me, maybe even kill me,
I'm still happier."

"Me, too," he admitted. Although he certainly wasn't settled when he let his mind drift
back to the feelings he'd had when he'd approached her overturned SUV. Over the years,
he'd investigated accident scenes. Every cop
had. And some of them had been gruesome.
And as family members and loved ones had
arrived, he'd seen the tears, the anguish. He'd
thought he'd understood. Now he wasn't so
sure.

Bone-deep fear was an interesting emotion.

He kissed the back of her neck. "I asked
Dawson to quietly investigate blue, black or
gray SUVs registered to male drivers within
a 30-mile radius of Ravesville. I didn't figure
that Gary Blake was going to do that."

"Thank you," she said. "Now I'm going to
get up and make some dinner."

He cupped her breast, ran the pad of his
thumb across her nipple. With his other hand,
he pulled her tight up against his erection.
"How hungry are you?"

She turned in his arms and kissed him, her
tongue in his mouth. "Very," she murmured.

He flipped her on her back and entered her

with one sharp thrust. She let out a sigh of pleasure. "Dinner can wait," she whispered and he began to move.

THE NEXT DAY, Chase went back up on the roof and started shingling in earnest. Around three in the afternoon, he saw Gordy Fitzler's truck turn into the driveway. He got off the roof and met the man as he got out of his truck.

"I heard about your wife's accident in town. I hope she's okay."

"She's good. Thanks for asking."

"Lucky girl," Gordy said.

It reminded him of what he'd said when he and Dawson had first discussed Lorraine Taylor. She'd been lucky a couple times now. When was that luck going to run out?

"You're making good progress," Gordy said.

"Good product," he said, trying to focus on the pallets of shingles that were still on the ground. It was his job to make sure that Raney's luck didn't run out.

"My son-in-law and daughter are doing a good job," Gordy agreed. "Speaking of them, that's why I'm here. I turn seventy-five tomorrow and tonight my kids are set on having a big party for me at the Wright Here, Wright Now Café. When I mentioned to them that I'd seen you, they told me that there's still room for a couple more before we start to have trouble with the fire marshal for overcrowding the place. I know it's very late notice but I'd be pleased to have you and your wife attend."

This man had made a difference in his life. He wanted to go. The possibility that someone had deliberately tried to harm Raney hung over his head. But he would be by her side. And she loved getting out, having the freedom to go somewhere. "We'd be honored," he said.

Gordy's face broke out into a big smile. He took off his ball cap and wiped the sweat off his forehead with the back of his hand. "Six o'clock. Come hungry. I hear the Wright sisters are going to make it something special. And no gifts. I've got my children and grandchildren, everything a man could ever want."

THERE WAS SOMETHING very comforting about being in the big old house and listening to Chase and his nail gun on the roof. *Tap, tap, tap. Tap, tap, tap.*

She was tackling her own project with vigor, very grateful for the big garbage cans that Chase had provided. While it felt odd to go through someone else's things, she hadn't found it as difficult to do as she'd anticipated. If it was something that she thought someone else could get some use out of, she put it in the keep-and-give-away pile. Otherwise, it was garbage. There were only a few exceptions that made her pause.

She heard the front door open and quickly walked into the kitchen. She was standing at the stove making a cup of tea by the time Chase took off his work boots and walked in.

"How's it going?" he asked.

"Good. How's the roof?"

"Big and steep. Other than that, fabulous." He reached for the cookies that she'd pulled from the oven just ten minutes earlier. "These look better than fabulous."

"They may be hot still."

He opened the refrigerator and poured a big glass of milk. He ate the first cookie in three bites. "Oh, these are good."

She smiled. So far Chase had eaten everything she'd made with gusto. She could probably mix straw with honey and bake it and he'd proclaim it the best yet.

"Gordy Fitzler just stopped by."

"To check on your progress?"

"I'm sure. Plus he wanted to invite us to his birthday party tonight at the Wright Here, Wright Now Café. His kids are throwing it for him."

She looked at him. "That's sweet."

"I thought we might go. If you didn't have other plans."

She wasn't exactly in the position to be making plans. But she didn't dismiss the comment. For the first time, it seemed as if Chase was tentative, not completely sure. Was it because this was almost like a date?

"No other plans," she said. "Will it be safe?"

"I wouldn't go if I didn't think so."

"We don't have a gift."

"He said no gifts."

She considered this. "Maybe we could make a charitable donation in his name to something that he supports."

Chase didn't even have to think about it. "He's always supported the local park district. When I was in high school, he donated over half the funds needed to put in the first swimming pool so that kids would have someplace to go in the summer. He's still wearing his Ravesville Park District ball cap."

"Sounds perfect."

"Can we talk about the rules for a minute?" he asked.

"Rules?"

He waved his hand. "Expectations. Firm expectations. We remain in visual contact at all times. That means you don't even step outside for a quick breath of fresh air without me. If you have to go to the bathroom, I'll check it first and then stand outside the door."

"I know we're supposed to be newlyweds but won't people think that's just a little over the top?"

"I'll do it in a way that people won't even notice."

She thought he perhaps underestimated how closely every woman's eyes in the place would follow him. He was just so darn handsome, so darn male. "Got it. Visual contact. At all times. It's just that I'm a little disappointed."

"Why?" He looked very concerned.

She lowered her lashes. "Well, Detective Hollister, that wasn't the only kind of contact I was hoping for tonight."

Shaking his head, he got up and pushed his chair back. He leaned close, his breath warm on her neck. "Don't you worry," he muttered. "As soon as the cake is served, you better be ready."

FIVE HOURS LATER, Chase stood in the living room, waiting for Raney. She was excited about the birthday party. He could tell. It made him realize that she'd steeled herself to several more weeks of house arrest and this was a welcome respite.

When he'd come in a half hour ago, she'd

been finishing up her painting in the kitchen. She was, he thought, about the slowest painter he'd ever seen. He could whip through a room in a couple hours and she'd been working for two days on one wall. But it gave her something to do and he was happy enough to let her plod along.

He'd grabbed clean clothes and gone upstairs to shower. Even though he was sleeping in her bed, it seemed too big a jump to move his clothes into her space. It would require a discussion and right now, that was the one thing that neither one of them wanted to have.

He understood his own reasons. He was conflicted as hell. He liked Raney. A lot. But he suspected that she was looking for what most women were looking for—a husband, someone who was willing to sign on for the long term. That wasn't him. He was ultimately going to disappoint her.

Why she didn't seem to want to talk about the future was a mystery to him. She'd been married. That had to mean that she believed in marriage. She didn't seem terribly angry or bitter about her divorce. And so like a good detective he watched and listened for clues, but so far she wasn't showing her cards.

When she came downstairs, he almost showed his whole hand. She looked incredible. While she wasn't overly tall, she had nice long legs that were looking really good in her black skirt. She had on a white silky-looking tank that he was itching to touch and put his hands under. "You're beautiful," he said.

"You're looking pretty good yourself."

He wore khakis and a loose tan shirt that would make it easy for him to carry his gun undetected.

"What time do we need to leave?" she asked.

He looked at his watch. "We have a few minutes."

"Good. I…uh…need to tell you something."

As quick as that, he saw his world changing. She was going to tell him that she'd thought it over and it had been one big mistake. A rush of disappointment filled him.

"Okay," he said.

He sat down on the couch and motioned for her to take the chair. He'd been disappointed before and survived it.

"I saw something the other day and it's weighing heavily on my mind."

She couldn't be talking about his injury. They'd had that discussion.

"I should have said something but I'm fairly confident that the person involved doesn't want that."

He was lost. But he did know that she was

truly worried that she was doing the right thing. He didn't say anything. She needed to work through this.

"When I was in the café the other day, before the accident, Summer was clearing a table and her shirt rode up. I saw her back and she had a big bruise on it. An old bruise, maybe a couple weeks old." She waved her hand. "I... I've become sort of an expert on the various iterations of bruised flesh."

That made his stomach hurt. "Did you ask her about it?"

"No. Sheila was there and I certainly didn't want her hearing the conversation, and I got the feeling that Summer was very sorry that I caught a glimpse. She didn't want to talk about it."

"There could be a thousand ways that somebody gets a bruise on their back."

"I know," she said. "That's what I kept thinking about. It's why I didn't say anything to begin with. But...it looked a great deal like the bruises I had from Harry Malone's shoe when he kicked me. I just can't get it out of my head that someone kicked her. Hard."

The picture he'd seen of Raney in her file, drawn, drained, beaten down, flashed in his head. She hadn't deserved that. No other woman deserved that and he felt a special affinity toward Summer. His brother had almost married her. What would Bray want him to do?

That answer was pretty clear. Bray fought the war on drugs because he hated the fact that the big-money punks were living large at the expense of the masses hooked on bad product. He risked his life every day to save the unknown thirteen-year-old from dying of a heroin overdose.

"I'll talk to her," he said. "Tonight."

Raney shook her head. "No. I want to do that. But I wanted you to know, because if she is in trouble, we may need your help."

BOTH OF THE Wright sisters were working. Trish, wearing a chef's hat and holding a big knife, was carving meat. She was smiling and laughing and delightfully entertaining people as they went through the line.

Summer was greeting guests. A young man of about fourteen who looked bored to death and a girl, maybe five, who was so excited she could barely stand still, were next to her. It wasn't a leap to assume they were her children. Same skin tone, same shape of the eyes. The boy had dark hair and the little girl's hair was a beautiful strawberry blonde.

It made sense that her children were there. She was a single mom who normally didn't work nights. She probably hadn't wanted to leave her kids at home alone.

They'd placed a sign on the door that said Closed for Special Event but Raney thought it probably didn't matter. Based on the crowd, she suspected all their regular customers were on the guest list.

The café looked very different. Small twinkling lights had been hung from the ceiling and strung across the room. The regular lights had been turned down. Every table had a cream-colored tablecloth with a vase of fall flowers as well as candles.

There was music playing and they'd left space for a small dance floor.

It wasn't New York fancy but rather, small-town nice.

She loved it.

They'd set the food on the counter and there was so much of it, it covered the entire length. Extra tables had been added, making it a challenge to circulate around the space. Not that that bothered Raney. She knew only a handful of people.

Mr. Fitzler, accompanied by two women she assumed were his daughters, probably in their late thirties or early forties, approached. They greeted Chase warmly and when he introduced her, they seemed delighted that she was there. "Thank you for inviting us," she said.

Reneta, the oldest one, waved a hand. "Chase is practically family. The son my father never had," she added good-naturedly. "We've got some empty chairs at our table, please join us."

It wasn't until she sat down that she saw Gary Blake in the far corner. He was out of uniform and had a beer in his hand. There were two other men with him and while they were talking animatedly and loudly, Gary was mostly staring in the direction of the far wall. At first, Raney thought he might be looking at his ex-wife and children. But that wasn't it. No, it was definitely the door. She leaned toward Chase. "Did you see Gary Blake?"

"Yep. Want a glass of wine?"

"Sure." Of course Chase had seen him. He'd probably already checked out everybody in the room.

He brought her back a glass of white wine in a little plastic glass and a bottle of water for himself. Then they started through the long line and filled their plates with roast beef, ham, mashed potatoes, roasted vegetables, all kinds of salads and finally homemade rolls.

Raney was almost done eating when the door opened and Sheila Stanton came in. She was alone. Raney saw Gordy's daughters exchange a look, and it wasn't one of pleasure.

Reneta leaned toward Chase. "You remember Sheila, Chase?"

"I do."

He wasn't giving anything away.

"She's a very good customer," Reneta explained. "Owns over half the commercial properties in Ravesville and uses us exclusively for roof work. My husband thought it was important that we invite her."

The underlying message was clear. If it had been up to the daughters, they'd have done something very different. Raney watched as Summer handed Sheila a plastic glass of wine. Sheila took a sip and made a face. Summer ignored it.

That was what Raney should do, too. Ignore Sheila Stanton. She turned the other way and struck up a conversation with Reneta's husband, who had assumed the roofing business. Within ten minutes, she had convinced Jonah to interview Keith for the entry-level office administrator position that was available at the company.

When Chase overheard the conversation, he leaned in. "I thought Keith wanted his own restaurant. Unless Fitzler's is putting a roof on the building, I'm not seeing the connection."

"Keith is a wonderful waiter and there's no doubt that he understands the customer service component. But to be a successful entrepreneur, he needs more general knowledge of how a business works. That knowledge can come from lots of places, including an office administrator job for a large roofing contractor. He wants to stay in the area. There aren't a lot of jobs that will put him on the right path. This one looks like a win-win. He wants to work for several years to save money to qualify for a loan. This would allow him to do that. And Fitzler's gets a good employee who is willing to work hard and learn."

"You're pretty damn smart," he said. She felt warm inside.

"Not so…" She caught a glimpse of Sheila Stanton, who was seated at a table across the room. She'd pushed one side of her hair behind her ear and Raney could see her chin. "Oh, my God," she said.

"What?" Chase asked.

She could tell that he was about to reach for his gun. She put her hand on his arm. "Smart. Not so smart. Chase, I think it might have been Sheila driving the SUV that pushed me off the road."

He blinked. "You said it was a man."

"I know, I did. And I thought it was. I saw facial hair. A glimpse but I was sure I'd seen it. But it's her chin. I know it is."

Chapter Thirteen

Chase was grateful he hadn't been drinking. Otherwise, the whirling in his head might have made him vomit on his shoes. What was Raney saying? Was it even possible?

When Sheila had left the grocery store that morning, he'd caught a glimpse of her car pulling out of the parking lot. She drove a black Lexus SUV.

Would Sheila have done something like this? It was crazy. They hadn't dated for more than ten years. She'd been married and divorced. He was *currently* married. Or at least she thought so. Surely she couldn't still be thinking there was a chance of a reconciliation.

But then he thought about the times that Cal had claimed to have seen her. He thought about the crazy letter. He thought about her staking out the grocery store in anticipation that he'd be shopping.

"Stay here," he said.

Sheila was getting a drink when she saw him approaching. "Chase," she said. "Lovely to see you."

"May I talk to you?" he asked. He was surprised at how level his voice was. He wanted to wring her neck if she was the one. But if Raney was right, and she'd taken the time to don a disguise, including facial hair, the crime had been premeditated and Sheila might be very dangerous indeed.

"Of course. Shall we step outside? It's such a beautiful night."

Visual contact at all times. He wasn't going to be the one to break the rules. "Over here should be fine," he said, leading her to the far corner of the room. He stood so that he could see Raney over Sheila's shoulder.

"My wife had an accident the other day," he said.

"I heard that. How is she?"

"Fine."

"A black SUV forced her off the road."

"Really?"

She was good. She didn't even look nervous. "You drive a black SUV."

She nodded. "A lovely one." She took a delicate sip of her wine. "Are you having this same conversation with everyone who drives an SUV or specifically with me?"

Her tone was suggestive, as if she liked that she'd perhaps been singled out. It took him one step closer to losing his dinner.

"Listen to me, Sheila. Whatever you and I had is long over. We both went our separate ways. I'm married. And I love my wife. I..." He faltered. *I love my wife.* He did. He really did. He took a breath. Steadied himself. "I don't want to see anything happen to her. If she so much as breaks a fingernail, I'll be upset. And I'll hunt down the person responsible. I will make sure they pay." He paused. "Do you understand, Sheila?"

"You're a fool, Chase Hollister," she said, her facade finally cracking. "I am twice the woman that she could even hope to be."

He was not going to defend Raney. She did not need to be defended. "I'm going to ask this question, just once. Were you driving the SUV that forced Raney off the road?"

"Of course I wasn't," she said.

He really couldn't tell if she was lying or not.

"You've been warned, Sheila. Don't forget it."

As Chase walked away, he could feel her eyes on his back. When he got back to the table, Raney's eyes were full of questions.

"I don't know how I ever thought she was desirable. Or sexy."

"You were nineteen. A jackrabbit in a dress might have done it for you."

He laughed so hard that the other people at the table started giving him odd looks. He looked at her plate. She'd cut her ham into teeny-tiny pieces, so small that it would fall through the tines of the fork if she tried to eat it. "Mad at the ham?"

"When I'm nervous, I need something to do with my hands."

He'd give her something to do with her hands. "Let's go home."

"I need to talk to Summer." She got up.

Chase let her go. He watched her walk across the room.

SUMMER WAS STILL BARTENDING, handing out little plastic glasses of red or white wine and twisting tops off bottles of beer. She smiled at Raney. "How was your dinner?"

"Wonderful," Raney said. "I'll have the chardonnay, please."

Summer poured it and handed it to her. Raney took it. There was nobody behind her in line. "Would you have just a minute that we could talk?"

She could tell that Summer was about to say no.

"Please," Raney added.

Summer stepped out from behind the table that had been set up as a makeshift bar. She glanced around the room. It was full of people. "Follow me to the kitchen," she said.

Chase had told her not to go outside alone. He hadn't said anything about the kitchen. As she crossed the room, she made eye contact with him and nodded toward the kitchen.

He gave her a sharp nod in response. She suspected he'd be waiting outside the door when she and Summer finished their conversation.

At the far end of the kitchen, a young man, maybe sixteen, was washing dishes using a big stainless-steel commercial dishwasher. He had earbuds in, listening to something.

"We can talk here," Summer said quietly. "Jess won't pay any attention to us."

Raney decided not to waste any time. "The other day, when your shirt pulled up, I saw what appeared to be a big bruise on your back. It didn't seem to be the kind of bruise that somebody would easily get. Unless...unless somebody had deliberately tried to hurt them. I was...am concerned about you."

Summer chewed on her upper lip. "I know that you mean well. I do. But I'm begging you, don't say anything to anybody about it. It could be very bad for me. For my children." Her eyes filled with tears. "Please."

She could feel the woman's desperation. "Can your sister help you?"

"No. She can't know. You cannot tell her."

"There are people who would help you. People like Chase."

Summer shook her head. "Please," she said again. "Things are better. I can't rock the boat now."

Raney reached for the cell phone that was in Summer's shirt pocket. She tapped on the keypad and entered her name and phone number. "Promise me that you'll call me if you need help. Anytime." She knew that she was just going to be in Ravesville for another three weeks but even after she left, she would do what she could.

"I promise," Summer said.

Raney didn't know if she meant it or if she was simply trying to end the conversation. Raney turned and left the kitchen. Summer didn't follow. As she had suspected, Chase was near the kitchen door. She realized that he'd been able to see into the kitchen through the small window in the door. He'd made good to keep her in his sights the whole night.

"Well?" he asked.

"She begged me to forget that I saw it."

"And what do you intend to do?"

"I have to do that. She's a grown woman. I gave her a chance to reach out for help. Either she's got the situation under control or she's not ready. Either way, I can't force it."

Chase nodded. "You're probably right. You know, you never cease to impress me. That took some guts to have that conversation with her. It could have gotten ugly real quick, but you were willing to take the chance."

"Channeling blonde Raney," she said, not thinking.

He pulled back. "What's that mean?"

She was embarrassed. But she knew Chase well enough to know that he wasn't going to let it go. "My new haircut and color was a little surprising. It made me look different. Feel different. Blonde Raney was adventuresome. Brave. Not afraid of the dark. Whole. I liked her. And when situations came up and I had to make a choice about how I was going to respond, I could either be blonde Raney or real Raney."

He studied her. "I like your hair. I already told you that. But you don't get your chutzpah from your hair, honey. It's part of you. You weren't blonde when you were traipsing down to the prison to help inmates polish their job-seeking skills. You weren't blonde when you outsmarted a madman and figured out a way to use washers from a filing cabinet to escape. You weren't blonde when you agreed to testify."

"It was blonde Raney who slept with you," she whispered.

He didn't say anything for a long minute. "Raney, you're an amazing person. You went through something really awful, something that no one should have to endure. But you survived. And I know you feel bad because Malone fooled you. And that destroyed your confidence, in others and in yourself."

He reached for her hand. "You know what the blond hair is. It's a crutch. Not in a bad way. Everybody needs a crutch once in a while. If you'd broken your leg, you'd have used a crutch without any thought. This isn't that different. Maybe it wasn't a physical break but you got shook, Raney. Understandably so. And you made some bargains with God. And now that you're free, it's scary because now you have the chance to keep those bargains. So it's easier to tell yourself that it's blonde Raney. But it's you, darling. All you."

She thought her heart might burst it was so full of love.

He leaned forward. "And you'd have slept

with me, regardless. I know it and you know it. We were meant to be together."

At that moment, Gordy Fitzler approached. "Chase, may I dance with your wife?"

"You have to ask her."

He extended an age-spotted hand in her direction. How could she refuse? "I'd love to," she said.

The music was a country hit from a few years earlier, just right for a slow dance with a dear man. "Thank you for letting us come to your party," she said. She meant it. It had been a wonderful night.

"I can tell that you're good for Chase."

It dimmed the glow of the night to know that she was deceiving this good man, all these people. "Thank you," she managed. She heard a disturbance near the door and looked over Gordy's shoulder.

Lloyd Doogan had come in. He was staggering and talking loudly. Fortunately the crowd had thinned considerably. Sheila had left shortly after Chase had talked to her. She looked around for Gary Blake. She did not want Lloyd arrested again. She didn't see the man and assumed he'd left while she was in the kitchen.

She saw Chase turn away from Hank Beaumont, the fireman who'd assisted her at the scene. Gordy stopped dancing and took a step toward Lloyd. Chase passed him before he could make much progress. "Enjoy your dance. I'll deal with this."

"Hey, Lloyd," Chase said, wrapping an arm around his shoulder. "How about you call it a night?"

"Got to wish Gordy a slappy birthday," he said, slurring his words as he tried to get away from Chase.

"Maybe tomorrow," Chase said.

Lloyd turned his head, so that he could look Chase in the eye. "He's a good man."

Chase nodded slowly. "Yes, yes he is. Okay, I'll go with you."

Together, the men crossed the room. One smart, confident and able. The other, less so, but determined to pay his respects to Gordy.

Gordy was gracious and shook Lloyd's hand. Then he leaned close to his son-in-law's ear. The man nodded and pulled his car keys from his pocket. Chase saw what was happening and handed Lloyd off to the man. They walked out the door and Raney assumed that Lloyd would be safely driven back to his apartment to sleep it off.

What could have gone very badly had ended up fine. Due in large part to how Chase had reacted. He took care of things. Took care of people.

It was one of the reasons she loved him.

Yes. Loved. She went back to dancing with Gordy and thought about what that could possibly mean. He hadn't said a word about what would become of them after the trial, when she'd be free to return to her old life in Miami.

He'd said that he'd never marry. Could she accept that?

No. While her first marriage hadn't gone so well, it hadn't soured her on the institution. She had learned a few things. She and Mike had wanted very different things. She wouldn't make that mistake again.

She wanted... She looked around the room. She wanted this. A town where people knew each other. They came out to celebrate significant events, they bought candy they didn't want so that the pom-pom girls could go to camp, they got clean cars washed again so that their elderly neighbors could afford heat in the winter.

She'd lost her parents at a young age. She wanted family.

Chase didn't want that kind of permanency. He was the guy who was only willing to sign a six-month lease, in the event that he wanted to move on.

It was so terribly sad.

The song ended and Chase came back over. He shook Gordy's hand and Raney leaned in and kissed the older man's cheek. Once Gordy had walked away, Chase pulled her close. "Are you ready to go?" he asked.

His intent was clear. And in her heart, she accepted that it would not be forever. But she had now. Right now. "I don't know," she said. "I was thinking about another piece of cake."

"No. I have been a patient man but I want to get my hands under that shirt. Let's go home."

She nodded. It might only be her home for three more weeks but she was going to make the best of it. And that included being in Chase Hollister's bed.

Chapter Fourteen

It was four days later when Chase's cell phone rang. They were both downstairs, getting ready to make breakfast.

He looked at the number. "Dawson," he told her and pushed a button. "Hey," he answered, his posture relaxed.

Within seconds that changed. He stood up and walked over to the back door of the kitchen. He wasn't saying much, just listening intently.

But Raney knew. Something bad had happened.

The call ended. He turned. His eyes were hard.

"What?" she said.

"Luis Vincenze was found dead this morning. His throat had been cut. He's been dead for a while. Probably for longer than a week."

So maybe shortly after he'd accompanied her to Missouri. The possibilities of what this might mean settled on her heart, making her chest feel heavy. "Someone killed him to get information on me," she said.

"We don't know that for sure," Chase corrected.

"But it's a possibility."

"Of course it's a possibility," he said, sounding angry. She knew it wasn't directed at her. It was the whole terrible situation. Poor Luis. He had just been doing his job.

"But it's also possible that it was some other jerk who had a beef with him. He was a cop. Had been one for more than twenty years. You make a lot of enemies in that amount of time."

That was true. But she knew, just knew, that it was related to her. "How is it that he could have been missing for more than a week and nobody reported it?"

"The afternoon he left you in St. Louis, he left a voice mail on his wife's cell phone, telling her not to worry, that he was being pulled to do some undercover work on a case and that he'd be out of contact for several days. He also left a message on his boss's office phone, telling him that he'd decided to use some of his vacation time now that he'd safely handed you off. Nobody got suspicious until the wife got nervous after trying his cell phone multiple times. She called his boss. It took them another day to tie it to a report of a dead body found in a vacation rental in the Ozarks."

"Oh." She was glad they had not yet eaten. "I'm guessing he left those messages under duress."

Chase swallowed. "They didn't just cut his throat. They tortured him. For some time. I think we have to assume that he broke. Maybe just to end the misery if nothing else."

Outside, a barn swallow swooped down, coming near the kitchen window, causing Raney to jump. She told herself to calm down, to breathe deep, to think.

"So we don't know what he told them. Whoever did this."

"No."

"What do they want us to do?" she asked.

"To hunker down here. They're sending two officers to provide 24/7 protection. We aren't in this alone. *You* aren't in this alone."

No, Chase was in it deep, too. She glanced at his leg, his poor injured leg that he still favored at times after a hard day's work outside. He could be injured again. Much worse. She stood up suddenly. "No. I should go. Somewhere else. And tell no one."

Chase stared at her, his face getting red. But when he spoke, his voice was still calm. "Sit down, Raney. Nobody is going anywhere. Not you. Not me."

She didn't sit. She couldn't. Deep in her bones, she knew that Luis Vincenze's death was because of her. "Is it possible that he'd been bought by Malone?" she heard herself ask. She felt terrible even voicing the speculation but her mind kept going back to the change in his attitude when he'd had to deliver her to Missouri.

"Why would you say that?" Chase asked, smoothly moving into investigator, fact-finder mode.

"When I was at the safe house in Miami, he was kind and helpful and even somewhat conciliatory. That is not a characteristic that I normally associated with the cops that I worked with at Next Steps."

He gave her a half smile. "Keep going."

"Everything changed on the plane. Once we landed, he became distant and preoccupied. He should have been overjoyed to get out of babysitting duty. He was going to be able to go home and be with his family. I should have realized the disconnect earlier, but I'd been so steeped in my own misery over coming to Missouri that I maybe didn't see the forest for the trees."

"Tell me everything you remember."

She thought back. "I know that he didn't know our final destination. Once he received a text, we got in the cab and met Chief Bates."

"So he and the chief talked?"

"For less than a minute. Luis got back in the cab that we'd arrived in."

"Would he have seen that the two of you entered the hair salon?"

"I don't think so. We walked for at least a couple minutes, turning two corners."

Chase considered that. "I suppose there are two possibilities. That Vincenze was a dirty cop and he was supposed to make sure that you never safely arrived in Missouri. The opportunity to kill you never presented itself, at least not in any way that wouldn't make him the immediate suspect. So once he handed you off to Chief Bates, he was essentially a dead man. Probably knew that. Hence, the agitation."

Raney shook her head and pretended to be picking petals off a daisy. "Should I kill her? Should I not? Should I kill her? Should I not?"

He reached out to still her hands. "What was the word you used that one day? I know. *Conflicted.* I suspect he was conflicted. The two of you had been close for almost two weeks. I suspect he probably liked you, thought you were a nice person. And maybe he couldn't see himself following orders."

"So he got killed because he didn't do his job?"

"Yeah. The other possibility is that he was a clean cop and Malone's people tortured him to get information on where you might be in St. Louis."

"And all he'd have been able to tell them is where he handed me off to Chief Bates. That wouldn't have been terribly helpful."

"No," he agreed.

A terrifying thought dawned on her. "You have to call Chief Bates. Right now. He's the linchpin that ties this all together. They'll go after him next."

"It's possible, but don't worry. The chief can take care of himself. But I think you're on the right path. Even if Vincenze was dirty, he never saw me, never heard my name. There's still no way for them to connect Lorraine Taylor to Raney Hollister."

For the first time since the telephone had rung, she could feel her breath coming easier. He was right. There was no need to panic. "What happens next?"

"We're going to have company. They should arrive in about an hour."

She thought about what that would mean.

"We're not going to be able to...be together. Not while they're here." Of course not. It could ruin Chase's career if it got back to the chief that he'd slept with the witness. That was not what the chief had likely been thinking when he'd set up this fictional marriage.

Chase shook his head, looking miserable. "No. You'll stay inside, away from any windows. I'll work with the other two officers and between the three of us, we'll keep one at the front and one at the rear of the house, 24/7. We'll rotate shifts so that we can grab some sleep."

Raney looked at her watch. "We will, however, be able to eat while they're here."

Chase's sexy amber eyes softened. "Of course."

"Maybe we should do the things now that we won't be able to do later?"

"Are you propositioning me, Mrs. Hollister?"

"I am merely asking if you can rearrange your schedule. Perhaps you could wait till later to eat? Say midmorning."

He took her hand and pulled her out of the chair. "I've always been fond of brunch."

CHASE LAY ON the bed, Raney lazily stroking his injured leg. It tickled but not enough to tell her to stop. He loved having her hands on him, loved the feel of her heat seeping into his body.

She moved her hands up the side of his body. To his ribs. Suddenly, her fingers stopped. She lifted her head. He tensed.

"Is this another bullet hole?" she asked, her tone a mixture of what he perceived to be disbelief and horror.

He shook his head and tried to pull her hand away.

She was stronger than she looked.

"What happened here?" she demanded.

And Chase considered lying. The scar was faint enough after all these years that no one had ever asked about it, but had they, he'd have had no compunction about telling them it was a birthmark or something else equally vanilla. But this was Raney.

"It's a cigarette burn," he said.

He felt her stiffen in his arm. "How did that happen?" she asked finally, her voice soft.

"My stepfather, Brick Doogan."

She raised up on one elbow, so that she could look at him. "How old were you?"

He thought a minute. "Seventeen."

She frowned and didn't say anything. He could practically see the wheels churning in her head. She was a fighter; she'd proved that time and time again.

Chase cleared his throat. "I suspect that you're wondering why a healthy seventeen-year-old boy would let someone do that to him."

"Maybe," she admitted.

"Because he told me if I didn't sit still and take it like a man, he was going to go get Cal."

Now she sat up in bed and pulled the sheet up to cover herself. She'd obviously decided this was not the kind of conversation one had naked.

"That makes no sense," she said.

He shrugged. "Shortly after Brick Doogan married my mother and moved in, I realized he was a bad guy. I was a dumb sixteen-year-old and I got busted for skipping school. I was making all As and Bs so it shouldn't have been a big deal, but he beat the hell out of me. I didn't have anybody I felt that I could turn to. Bray, who is four years older, had already enlisted and was halfway around the world. Cal was just thirteen."

"What did your mother say?"

"I didn't tell her. She had been so sad when my dad died. And for two years, I would hear her crying in her bed. Once she met Brick, she stopped crying. I'll never know what she saw in the man but she was happy. At least at first. I didn't want to ruin it."

"That's a big burden for a sixteen-year-old."

"Yeah. I got over the beating and almost forgot about it. But then it happened again. We'd let a couple goats loose in the high school. It got people pretty excited."

She smiled.

"That was the cigarette burn." It had been seventeen years, but he could still feel the startling pain of having his flesh burned.

She reached out her arm, lightly rubbed her fingers over the scarred skin. "I'm sorry," she whispered.

He drew in a breath. "It was a third-degree burn. It got infected and I started running a raging fever. I had to tell my mother."

"What did she say?"

Now came the hard part. "She told me to tell the doctor in the emergency room that I'd been smoking and fallen asleep on my cigarette."

Raney was silent for a long minute. "Did you?"

He nodded. "Not for him. For her."

"I'm sorry your mother is dead, and I know that you're never supposed to talk badly about the dead, but that just seems awful. Yet you don't talk about your mother as if she was awful."

"She wasn't awful. She was weak and needy

and when my father died, I think overwhelmed
with the idea of raising three boys on her own."

"Did Brick mistreat her?"

"No. Not to my knowledge. It was always
me. Until it was Calvin. And that's when I
knew things had to change."

"I don't understand."

"My senior year of high school, our football
team went to the state championship. I was a
starting running back and it was pretty cool.
My mother, Cal and Brick were all at the game.
And we won. Everybody was pretty happy.
What I didn't realize was that all the parents
went out drinking afterward, celebrating their
kids' achievement. The players were all invited
back to the quarterback's house. His parents
had a bunch of money and they had an indoor
pool and a game room. We stayed the whole
weekend. There was no way to say no to the
invitation and besides, I wanted to go."

"You were a kid."

"Yeah. But I was worried about being away
from home. And I warned Cal to watch out for
Brick. If I'd known that he was going drinking, I'd have never stayed away. He was always
meaner when he was drinking."

"What happened?"

"He pushed Cal's hand through a window.
The one in the living room. It was cut up

enough that my mother had to take him to the emergency room for stitches."

"And even then, no one found out."

"Nope. Cal told them he tripped."

"Why?" she whispered.

"Because Brick told him that if he told the truth, that it would be worse the next time."

He watched her. She understood. Malone had also played the game of psychological warfare with her.

"Cal had just turned fifteen years old and he was small for his age. He was scared of Brick." He paused. "You should see him now. Former navy SEAL, six feet tall, all muscle."

"What happened when you got home?"

"I saw Cal's hand all bandaged up and went crazy. Went at Brick like a madman. He was a big, strong guy and outweighed me by forty pounds but I was winning when my mother tried to break up the fight. I didn't want her to get hurt so I stopped. And I thought, too, that this will be the end of it. She'll leave the bastard now."

"But she didn't?"

"No. And when I told her I was taking Cal, she said that I couldn't, that she would fight me."

"He was a minor. She was his mother," she said. "It would have been a battle, but surely the hospital records would have helped you. Couldn't you have confided in a teacher, a counselor, anybody?" she asked, sadness in her tone.

"Probably. But I didn't. I was ashamed. I thought this was the kind of thing that happened in poor, uneducated families. I wanted to be something. I didn't want this hanging over my head. Anyway, I wasn't leaving Cal alone with Brick. So I stayed. I worked like a dog and went to school at the same time to save enough money so that the two of us would have a place to live. We left the morning of Cal's eighteenth birthday. I got hired on by the St. Louis PD and, well, you pretty much know the rest."

He could tell she was puzzled about something. *Let it go*, he prayed. *Just let it go.*

"So after the incident with Cal, Brick reformed?" she asked.

She was so smart. She would have made a good cop. Knew just where the weak points of the story were.

"I told him that if he ever touched Cal or my mother, I would kill him. I think he believed me. And, every once in a while, I let him go at me."

"What?"

"I had figured him out. He was an unhappy

man. Mad that he was working in a factory, hated his bosses, thought they were all lazy. He wanted somebody to pay for his lot in life. And about every six months, he just couldn't hold the anger in. That's when I knew he'd be dangerous. When he'd start drinking and miss a couple days of work, I'd do something that I knew would make him angry and then he'd feel justified when he handed me my lunch."

She got out of bed, taking the sheet with her. "You made yourself a target?"

"I did. I never let him take another cigarette to me. I'd let him land a punch or two and then he'd kick me out of the house for a couple days."

"Where did you go?"

"Never far. If it was warm enough, I'd sleep in the hammock on the porch. If it was winter, I'd have to go to Fitzler's. I didn't like being that far away from Cal, although I knew that Brick wasn't going to touch him."

"How could you be sure?"

"Because even though he might land a punch, I think he knew by this time that I was strong enough and fast enough that if I decided to fight back, I would win."

She sat back down on the bed. Reached out her arm. "You protected everyone else but not yourself."

"In a way. But you have to understand, I didn't want to kill him. I would have but I didn't want to because he wasn't worth it. I thought I would go to jail and by that time, I'd decided that I wanted to be a cop. My life would have never turned out the way it has."

"And you never saw him after you left at age twenty-one?"

"I saw him when my mother was dying. She asked her hospice nurse to call us. Bray, Cal and I came home. We were at her bedside for a little over two days. He was around but didn't interact with us in any way."

"I imagine Cal feels a great deal of gratitude toward you. For protecting him."

He held up a finger. "This is important. Cal doesn't know. As far as he's concerned, Brick never laid another hand on either one of us."

"And your older brother?"

"The only thing he knows about is the time Cal's hand went through the window. That was enough for him to hate Brick Doogan forever. I never told him the rest. He'd have killed Doogan for sure and then I'd have lost a brother to the prison system."

She stared at him. "You're amazingly well adjusted. Considering."

"I had to let it go. On her deathbed, my

mother asked to speak to me privately. She asked for my forgiveness. And I gave it to her."

He looked at his watch. "We need to get up. They'll be here soon."

She didn't argue. Just dropped her sheet and hurriedly stepped into her clothes. But when she turned her head, he thought he caught the sheen of tears in her eyes.

Chapter Fifteen

Chase might have forgiven his mother, which she thought was pretty damn amazing given the circumstances, but he hadn't escaped unscathed. There were more scars than the one he bore on his chest.

So many things made sense now. His ability to stay calm, no matter what. He would not have let Brick know that he was getting to him.

His reluctance to sign more than a six-month lease and his comments that people needed to be ready to change jobs at a moment's notice, even though he'd been at the same job for thirteen years. Chase had not been free to go before and now he told himself he was ready to leave at any time.

His unwillingness to marry. He'd been taking care of his family for years, making sacrifices beyond any a young man should have to make. He was done.

It was heartbreaking, it really was.

A lesser man would not have endured it and come out whole.

RANEY WAS PAINTING the kitchen when their two new bodyguards arrived. Chase knew both men and made the introductions. Leo was in his early fifties with a face that had been pockmarked by teenage acne. He wore a white shirt with frayed cuffs that looked as if it had been washed too many times. His voice was gruff and he had a pack of cigarettes in his pocket.

Toby was twenty years younger, thin and wearing a lovely green sweater that was way too warm for the day. He pointed to the fresh paint on the wall. "Oh, that's nice. It picks up the natural light from the window. I'm in the middle of a big remodeling project myself." He walked over to look at the can. "Toasted Meringue. Excellent choice."

Raney lifted her nose in the air—just slightly. Not enough that the two new arrivals would think she was odd but enough that Chase would understand that others recognized good taste.

Chase rolled his eyes.

"Come see what I got for the living room," she said. Toby started to obediently follow.

"We're not filming an episode of HGTV here," Chase said, rolling his eyes.

Toby blushed and sat down. Leo looked around, probably in hopes of seeing an ashtray. When he didn't, he started nervously rubbing the edge of his thumb on the corner of the table.

Raney took pity on both men and pushed some warm coffee cake in their direction.

Within minutes, Chase was briefing them on the assignment, showing them entrances, exits and going over their daily schedule.

They decided that Chase and Toby would take the first watch, leaving Leo inside to rest until it was his turn. At first Raney felt self-conscious about having the man in the other room but soon got busy painting and forgot about him.

Midafternoon, Chase came in to get a drink. Leo got off the couch and went outside to take his place.

Chase looked at the walls in the kitchen and smiled. "It does look nice," he said.

She knew he was thinking that she'd made pitiful little progress and that she must be the slowest painter on earth. But she wasn't. She was actually pretty fast and had been making good progress—just not in the kitchen.

Now that he'd told her the story, she was even more pleased that she'd followed her instinct and decided to tackle Brick Doogan's bedroom. Initially, she'd done it because she thought it was crazy that Chase was sleeping on a couch with his legs hanging off the end when there was a perfectly good bed, albeit with a hideous bedspread.

Now she understood why Chase couldn't bring himself to handle the man's things. Now he wouldn't have to.

"How's it going?" she asked him, as he drank a big glass of water.

"Fine. I think it may be a good thing that I got the roof done. There's another storm coming." He put his glass on the counter. "Will you be okay upstairs by yourself?" he asked softly.

"Yes. I'll just make sure my window is closed so there are no fluttering curtains."

He swallowed hard. "I want you to know something. I'm really glad your curtains fluttered the last time."

It wasn't an expression of love or eternal commitment but it was something. "Me, too," she said.

They were both silent, too aware that strangers were outside. "It smells really good in here," he said finally.

"I made a lasagna for dinner."

"They would have eaten a sandwich."

"I know."

He smiled at her. "You like taking care of people."

Maybe they weren't so different in that way. "Are you going back out?"

"Yep. I'm on until six." He opened the door. They both heard the noise at the same time.

It was the chugging rumble of Lloyd's motor-cycle. Chase grabbed the walkie-talkie off his belt. "Approaching motorcycle. Not a threat. Stand by."

They had not seen Lloyd for four days, not since Gordy Fitzler's birthday party. They went to the front door and opened it. Lloyd parked his motorcycle and came in, none the wiser that eyes watched him from the heavy tree line.

"Hi, Lloyd," Raney said.

"Hello." He was wearing a backpack and shrugged to lower a strap. He did not look at Chase but Chase was watching him like a hawk.

Lloyd opened the zipper and pulled out something that was wrapped in yellowed tis-sue paper. He started unwrapping and Raney could see that it was not one thing but three things—three identical pictures, in three iden-tical frames.

"When I took the key off his dresser," he said, "I took these. They were in his bottom drawer."

The picture was of three young boys and a woman. She immediately recognized a much younger Chase. One boy would have been Bray and the younger, Cal. It was the woman who held Raney's attention. This was Chase's mother. Widowed young, raising three boys on her own, she'd been a pretty woman. It was easy to see where the boys had gotten their height.

She might not have been a bad woman but she had made terrible choices. She'd married a bad person.

Raney understood that on some level. After all, she'd chosen poorly, too. Not that Mike had been abusive, but they'd been too different. He wanted notoriety, even if it was only in the small community that followed professional surfing. He craved the next big wave, the thing that would set him apart.

She'd weighed him down because she was most happy living quietly. She didn't need or want public adoration. She liked permanence and he loved the adventure of a new beach.

But she'd owned up to her poor choice. They'd divorced and gone on with their lives.

She looked at the picture again. This woman had chosen to let her son pay the price for her flawed decision.

She watched Chase's reaction to the photo. Shock, then awe, before he pulled on his "you can't shake me" face.

What would make him smile again like the young man in this picture?

Certainly not staying in Ravesville. He'd left it and everyone in it behind thirteen years ago.

She turned the frame over. For Brayden. The other two were similarly inscribed: For Chase and For Calvin. "Your brothers are going to like this," she said.

Lloyd shifted from foot to foot. "I shouldn't have taken them."

"It's okay, Lloyd. No harm done," Chase said. "I appreciate you bringing them back."

"You don't think I stole them?" he asked.

Chase shook his head. "You borrowed them. It's different."

"I didn't remember that I had them until I heard Blake talking about you and your brothers."

Chase frowned. "Gary Blake? The police officer?"

Lloyd nodded. "After the party the other night. It was hot inside my place and I don't got no air-conditioning. I walked outside. And I overhead them talking."

"Overheard who?"

"Blake and that dark-haired bitch. She's so rich, treats everybody bad."

Raney looked at Chase. She was pretty sure she knew who Lloyd was talking about.

"Sheila Stanton?" Chase asked.

Lloyd nodded. "Those two were arguing, practically yelling."

Lloyd had been really drunk that night. How reliable was this information? She remembered what Chase had told her about small towns and how information flowed.

"What did they say?" she asked. She couldn't help it. Even if it was just gossip, she wanted to hear it. Sheila Stanton had been on her mind. And she didn't exactly know why. Of course it was true that her two encounters with the woman, first at the grocery store and then at the café, hadn't exactly been comfortable. But it was more than that.

The woman had been Chase's lover. For a long time. And now, especially after sharing his bed, perhaps Raney had sunk to a new low and was *comparing*. Her blond, somewhat un-ruly curls to Sheila's thick, glossy, perfectly shaped hair. Her medium height to Sheila's sleek, almost Amazonian stature. Her rather benign oval face to Sheila's high cheekbones and sculpted chin.

With a quick jerk, she put the picture down. There was always going to be someone pret-tier, more successful, richer, smarter. Chasing that was a small person's game and a waste of time. Even BHM, she hadn't been inclined to spend much time doing it. After Harry Malone, she simply wouldn't bother.

"Never mind," she said.

Chase held up a hand. "No. Go on, Lloyd."

"He was pointing his finger in her face. Said that he'd been married to one woman who'd loved a Hollister and that he didn't intend to waste time with somebody else who had the same problem."

Gary Blake and Sheila Stanton. Raney's head was whirling.

"Did you hear anything else?" Chase asked.

"She said something but I couldn't hear it. Then he told her that he didn't intend to let her take him down." Lloyd picked up the yellowed tissue paper and crumpled it in his big hands. "You better be careful around Blake. He can make things bad for you if he wants."

Chase nodded. "Thanks for letting me know, Lloyd. And if Blake starts to bother you, you come tell me, okay?"

Lloyd nodded, got his backpack situated again and opened the front door. Neither Raney nor Chase said anything until the sound of his motorcycle had completely faded away.

"Well, that's interesting," Chase said.

"He was drunk that night."

"Well lubed for sure. Sloppy, yeah. But incoherent, no. I suspect he heard it more or less accurately."

"What does it mean?" she asked.

"I think it means that Gary Blake and Sheila Stanton are involved in some way. But not publicly."

Raney put her hand up to her mouth. "I saw him staring at the door. I thought it was weird. I bet he was watching for her. Waiting."

Chase nodded. "Something else makes sense. And it actually makes me sort of happy."

Raney shook her head. "Okay, you lost me."

"When you had your accident, you told Blake that it was a black or blue SUV that got too close. He reacted to that."

"He did?"

"Yeah. Subtly but definitely a reaction. He knows that Sheila drives a black Lexus SUV. It wasn't until you said that it was a man that he relaxed."

"And that makes you happy because…?"

"Because it probably was Sheila. That means it wasn't Malone's hired guns. That's good."

"True. But don't you think it's bad that the police are letting her get away with it?"

Chase shrugged. "We don't know that for sure. Maybe Blake initially suspected Sheila, based on the fact that he has some knowledge of the fact that she's still…*infatuated* with me."

He ran his fingers through his hair. "I can't believe I just said that word. But once you said it was a man, he went down another path."

"In that case, he's not a dirty cop."

"Right. Stupid. But not necessarily dirty. What likely happened is that he saw me talking to Sheila. Probably got jealous, demanded to know what it was about. Maybe she told him. Then it could have gone one of two ways. Either she continued to deny it and he believed her or, more likely, she continued to deny it and he didn't believe her. Which maybe means he's not so stupid."

"Or she admitted it and he's continuing to stick by her," Raney said.

"Okay. We're back to stupid."

Raney smiled. "I like Lloyd. He's a nice guy. And it was good of him to return these photos."

Chase picked one up. "I think I was about twelve in this. My dad was still alive. He took the picture. We'd gone to some park for a picnic and my mother had said that we couldn't play until she got a picture." He paused. "That was a good day."

She stood on her tiptoes and kissed his forehead. "Keep those thoughts here. Push the other ones away. Far away."

He reached for her. "I wish to hell we were alone."

She let him hold her. In his arms, she felt safe. And it was wonderful.

But her gut told her that it was temporary, that things were about to change.

DUE TO THE need to have two people outside at all times and the way the shifts worked out, Chase stood outside in the dark while Raney was inside, eating lasagna with Toby.

He'd been crazy enough to get close to the windows once to look inside. They'd been sitting at the dining room table, paint samples in hand, staring at the far wall, likely in deep discussion about exactly how Sunset Wonder was going to look on the wall.

He was glad to be outside, alone with his thoughts. He could have stayed dry on the porch and had a place to sit but he'd chosen to walk the property, getting wet in the steady rain that had been falling for the past half hour.

Seeing that photo of his mother and brothers had been a surprise. He distinctly remembered posing for the picture but didn't think he'd ever seen the finished product. As a twelve-year-old boy, he wouldn't have thought to ask about it.

But his mother had saved it, had put away three copies, one for each of her sons. Had she done it right away? Or had that happened years later, after Brick Doogan had entered their lives? Had she perhaps found the pictures, decided they were a reflection of happier times and wanted her boys to have that memory?

He made another pass across the yard. Looked down the road, but it was raining too hard to see any lights at Fitzler's. Turning, he started back and realized there was a light in his own house where there should not have been.

Someone was in Brick's room. And for one crazy moment, he thought the man had come back. Then he grabbed hold of his senses and carefully approached. The heavy curtains hid most everything, but there was a sliver of light showing where the two panels came together. But it wasn't enough to see anything.

Had someone gotten into the house?

Someone who wanted to harm Raney?

He moved quickly but quietly. He eased open the front door, listened for Raney or Toby, didn't hear anything. The house was warm and smelled good, and when he saw that Toby and Raney had put a big strip of Sunset Wonder on the wall to test it out, his step faltered.

He pulled his gun. Got to the kitchen. Now he heard voices. Raney. Toby. Couldn't make out the words, but they didn't appear distressed.

Got to Brick's door. Listened. They were across the room, near the attached bath.

He swung around the corner, ready to shoot whoever he found there.

Chapter Sixteen

Chase almost dropped his damn gun.

Raney let out a squeak and Toby dropped the paint can he was holding. Fortunately, the lid was on.

The room had been completely emptied of its contents. The bed had been stripped down to the mattress. The closet doors were open, showing a clean space.

The walls had been painted. The ghastly gold had been replaced with the Prickly Pear Delight that he'd thought they were buying for the dining room. It looked totally different.

"How?" he managed.

Raney smiled. "I wanted to surprise you."

He walked farther into the room. She'd surprised him, all right. He struggled to maintain his composure, keenly aware that a fellow officer was standing in the room.

"Where did you put everything?" he asked.

She smiled. "It was tricky but I would wait

until I heard you on the other side of the roof and then I'd run a few bags out to the garage. You have a couple of very full garbage bins out there. Things I thought could be donated are in a bag, in the bathroom. I just...just didn't think you wanted to deal with this—" she glanced at Toby, who was clearly interested in the conversation "—this mess."

It was the nicest thing that anybody had ever done for him. When he'd talked to Raney, had finally opened up to someone about those years of living with Brick, the ever-present pressure in his chest had finally started to release. He would never have trusted anyone else with that secret. But he knew that he could trust her, knew that she wouldn't judge.

Knew that she would offer unconditional love.

Like this.

The hell with what information got back to anybody in the department or even the chief. "Toby, can we have a minute here?" he said.

The young man started to leave the room. But before he could get to the doorway, Chase's phone buzzed. He pulled it out, recognized the number and knew that it had to be bad.

"Hollister," he answered.

"This is Chief Bates. We've got a problem. We now have very good reason to believe that your location has been compromised. You need to bring Lorraine Taylor back in."

Chase walked to the window, lifted the edge of the heavy curtain with a finger. "Tell me what happened."

"There have been a string of robberies near Patch Street."

That was the street where he'd first met Raney, where she'd gotten her hair cut.

"Reports got taken by a couple different officers and we didn't piece things together as quickly as we should have."

He could hear the anger in the chief's voice.

"It wasn't until the yogurt shop got hit that the pattern was established," Chief Bates said. "Somebody had stolen security-camera footage from several of the mom-and-pop stores on that block."

Chase tried to tamp down the ringing in his ears. Vincenze had given up the drop location, maybe voluntarily, maybe under duress. Didn't matter. Once they had that, it was a simple matter of trying to identify where Raney had gone after that. And with who.

"You think they got enough to know that she went into the hair salon and then a couple hours later left with me?"

"We do. Based on the angles of the cameras."

"I didn't have a name tag on," he said, fighting for reason. "Even if they saw me, how would they know my name? How would they know that I was coming home to Ravesville?"

The chief paused. "Gavin Henderson is dead. Shot at close range after he'd taken a beating that produced very similar injuries to those found on Luis Vincenze."

Gavin Henderson. Chase felt sick. He was a good officer. A husband. A father. But it made sense. Gavin had arrived with his camera around his neck. While there were lots of police officers on the St. Louis PD, there were only a few police photographers. And only a few of them were male. It would not have taken someone very long to work through the list.

"I want you in your car in five minutes. If necessary, I'll put Lorraine in a cell if that's what it takes to keep her safe."

Let her stay here. He would keep her safe. But the chief's logic made more sense. Sure, they could send more officers to Ravesville, but that probably wasn't practical or cost-efficient. They certainly couldn't count on the local police department to be helpful. And no matter what argument Chase made, the chief was going to shoot it down. He wanted his witness where he could see her and to know that she was safe.

"All right. Expect us in two hours." Chase hung up and turned toward Raney.

"What's wrong?"

There was no time to cushion the blow, to soften the words. "That was Chief Bates. We're moving you. Now. This location has been compromised." He could spare her the details about Gavin Henderson. "You've got two minutes to throw some things in a suitcase."

"But—"

"Raney, please," he said.

She nodded and ran out of the room, past Toby, who still stood in the doorway.

Chase quietly told the officer about Henderson. "Raney and I will take one vehicle, you and Leo follow us." He used his cell phone to call Leo and quickly filled him in.

Then he set about gathering every one of the extra weapons that Dawson had brought. He separated the arsenal between himself and the other two officers.

By the time he was done, Raney was downstairs, her small suitcase with her. She'd put on a coat.

They walked out the door and the four of them got into the two vehicles.

Chase stuck his head out the window and

spoke to the other men. "Let's go. Keep close to me. Under no circumstances do we get separated."

CHASE HAD TURNED on the heat but still, Raney was shivering. She'd gotten soaked just running to the SUV. But it wasn't the rain that had her blood running cold.

The wind was blowing hard, rocking the SUV. When they turned left out of the lane, rather than right, which would have taken them into Ravesville, Raney had to resist pulling on Chase's arm.

She wanted to go to the Wright Here, Wright Now Café. She wanted to sit in the booth and order a hot chocolate and a piece of cherry pie with vanilla ice cream. *I'll be safe there.*

But she wouldn't be. And she'd be putting others in danger. The way she was putting Chase in danger right now.

"I'm sorry," she said.

He turned to look at her. "What are you talking about?"

"For all this. For getting you into this mess. I'm sorry they chose you."

He took one hand off the wheel and reached over to grab her hand. He brought it up to his lips, kissed it gently. "The Sunset Wonder is a perfect match for the fireplace. Just like you said."

She tried to jerk her hand back but he wouldn't let go. "You want to talk about paint colors now?" she asked, hardly believing it.

He smiled against her hand. Then he kissed it again. "I want to talk about paint colors and carpet samples and whether bronze or silver faucets would be better in the bathroom. I want to talk about the flowers that you'll plant and the rose bushes that I'll have to drag home from the store. I want to talk about our children and the noise they'll make running up and down the stairs."

"But your job?"

"I'll find another one," he said. "We belong together, Raney. We belong in Ravesville. Marry me, Raney."

She thought her heart might burst. She turned in her seat, to tell him that she loved him, and out of the corner of her eye saw something move.

"Watch out!" she yelled.

Chase floored it and got past the vehicle that was coming at them like a bat out of hell from the side road, its lights off.

They heard the crash and knew that Leo and Toby had not been as fortunate. Even the howling wind could not dull the horrific crunch of metal on metal.

"We have to go back!" she yelled.

"No. That was no accident." Chase took his cell phone out and tossed it in her lap. "Call 911. Tell them that there's a multivehicle accident with serious injuries at the intersection of Hawk and Billow."

Her fingers were shaking so badly that she could barely press the keys. But she managed it. She told the person on the other end exactly what Chase had told her to say. Then the 911 operator asked for her name.

"Raney. Raney Hollister," she whispered and ended the call.

Chase turned and looked at her. "Hang on, Raney. We're going to get out of this."

But that didn't seem too likely when up ahead, on the narrow dark road, their headlights picked up the shape of a vehicle parked horizontally across the road. They would have to go through it.

There was no place to go.

Chase whipped the vehicle to the right. They left the paved road, dipped down into the ditch then up again and they came out on the other side. They were in a field of corn that had been recently picked. They pounded over the roughness of the remaining short stalks, their SUV rocking. "We're going back the other way," Chase yelled.

He was making a big circle. They might make it. They just might.

And then they hit a low spot in the field and their tires sunk into the rain-soaked ground and they were stuck.

Chase flipped off his lights and threw open the door. It was still raining but there was some light coming from the full moon that was hidden by the clouds. He reached for Raney and hauled her out. "Run!" he yelled.

She thought he would go for the road but instead he pulled her farther into the field. She stumbled but he kept her upright and moving.

She risked a look behind her. The road was no longer dark. She saw lights and men and knew that they weren't going to make it.

She almost ran into the first tree before she realized that the field had given way to the woods. She could smell the wet foliage, got slapped in the face with a dripping branch.

They went maybe thirty more steps when Chase jerked her to a stop. "Get up into this tree," he said. "Don't make a sound. No matter what. And don't come down until I come back. Do you understand?"

He was leaving her. He was going to leave

her and draw their attention away from her. "No," she said. "We stay together."

He put both hands on her face and kissed her hard. It was desperate with need. "It's too dangerous. Listen to me. Do exactly what I say. They won't expect me to leave you." She felt movement and thought it might be him pulling something from his pocket. He pressed a gun into her hand. "Take this. It's ready to go. Just squeeze the trigger hard. If they see you, start shooting. Don't hesitate. Do you understand?"

She was crying. "Yes."

He kissed her again. "Give me your foot," he said, bending down.

He boosted her up into the tree. She felt for the branches and climbed. She'd told Chase that she wasn't afraid of heights, but with each foothold she became more and more terrified, knowing that she was truly alone. She got as high as she could go and tried to find a spot to rest her weight so that she could remain motionless.

She was wet and cold and her hands stung. She suspected they were bleeding. After a few minutes in the dark, she heard noise off to the left, deeper into the woods, and knew Chase was deliberately trying to lead their attackers away from her.

To her right, she heard crashing through the

trees, saw big lights as their pursuers hunted them down.

Felt them stop under her tree.

CHASE RAN FAST, not even attempting to be quiet. *Go. Go. Go.* The words pumped through him as he wrestled to stay upright when he skidded across rain-slicked tree roots and soft muddy patches. His injured leg felt the stress and cramped up in response. He pushed through the pain.

He prayed he wouldn't ram into a tree and knock himself out before he could get far enough away from Raney. He knew he couldn't outrun them. But that wasn't his intent. He just needed to get to a place where he had decent cover. He hadn't been able to get an accurate count but he thought there were at least two, maybe three. Not great odds but not horrific, either. If they split up, he could take a couple out at a time.

Of course, if they managed to neutralize him and discovered Raney wasn't with him, she would be in terrible danger.

He took a step, felt the ground give way and half slid, half stumbled down a sharp embankment. He landed in water that came up over his calves. Some kind of stream. He couldn't see a damn thing now. He plunged forward, hoping that it was narrow, hoping that he hadn't gotten disoriented and he was truly crossing the stream rather than walking the length of it.

He hit the opposite bank, let himself feel a moment of relief that he was out of the water and scrambled up the side. Once up on solid ground, he found a big tree and sank down behind it. He gulped in air as quietly as he could.

Now he needed the element of surprise.

He saw the bobbing and weaving of their light. He risked a look around the tree. He would have a good angle as they crested the bank. His only chance was if they put their high-powered flashlights on the ground while they pulled themselves up over the edge. If they didn't, their light would blind him and he wouldn't get his shot off.

He held his gun with both hands, willing his aim to be steady, sure. He heard them hit the water. Two separate splashes.

Heard one of them grunt and swear and then he didn't hear them in the water anymore. He counted to three. Moved from around the tree. Raised his gun.

Target One had put his flashlight down, exactly like Chase had hoped. The light was still on but at that level it wasn't blinding to Chase. He saw the man's head. Then his torso. Waited still.

Saw the second target come over the edge. No flashlight. Maybe he'd dropped his when he'd stumbled in the stream. He was big, and having difficulty pulling himself up over the bank.

Chase waited. One second. Two. The first target was reaching for his light. Chase fired. Saw the target fall backward.

Swung his gun fifteen degrees to the right. Fired again. Target Two took a step forward. Chase hit him with a second round. He went down.

Chase counted to ten, didn't sense any movement and cautiously moved away from his cover. The light at ground level was still shining. He hurried forward. There had been three, he was sure of it. He had to find him before the man found Raney.

When he approached the bodies, he picked up the flashlight and used his foot to flip the second target over. Looked at his face. Didn't recognize him. Checked his carotid pulse, made sure he was dead.

He shined his light down into the stream. Saw the first man. He'd landed on his back. Chase didn't bother checking his pulse. He could tell he was dead. His head was under-water.

Chase crossed the stream, flashlight in one

hand, gun in the other. He kept the flashlight pointed down, with his fingers spread over the lens, partially obscuring the light. He needed some help to see the way, to avoid making a misstep that would call attention to his location, and also to see the broken-off branches and other damage he'd caused as he'd charged through the forest. It was the only way he was going to find Raney's tree. He didn't know how far behind he'd left her. He'd thought he'd been running hard for at least five minutes before he'd slipped into the stream, but the terrain had been challenging so maybe a half mile at the most.

He couldn't go as quickly now. *Ten minutes, Raney. Ten minutes. Hang on.*

Chapter Seventeen

Chase had been walking for seven minutes when he heard a noise behind him. He threw himself sideways, managing to avoid the bullet that whizzed past him and hit a tree. He rolled and tried to get his own shot off but his gun was kicked out of his hand by a damn giant.

"Get up," the man said, his voice thick with an accent that Chase didn't recognize. The man picked up the flashlight that Chase had dropped and shone it in Chase's eyes. "Where is she?" the man asked.

"Who?" Chase asked.

The giant backhanded him. Chase hit the ground hard.

"Get up," the man snarled.

Chase did. Slowly.

"Where is she?"

"I have no idea."

The man swung his gun, catching Chase

on the side of his head. Chase went down to his knees.

"I will ask one more time. Then I will start shooting. Your elbows first. Those are very painful. Then your knees. And you will be helpless when the coyotes come and get you. Where is the woman?"

Chase tried to make it look as though he was considering the question. He was really trying to give his ears time to stop ringing. "I told her to run in the direction of the cabin."

"What cabin?"

"It's at the edge of the forest."

"I did not see any cabin."

"You have to know what you're looking for. I grew up in this area," Chase said, hoping the man knew that to be true. "I showed it to her earlier this week. Just in case. Listen, this is just an assignment for me. I've only got seven years until I can retire with twenty years. Just leave me here and go find her. Shoot me in the arm or something if you want to slow me down."

"Take me to the cabin. Then I will shoot you like you asked."

The giant would kill him. That was for sure. But he needed to lead him away from Raney and find an opportunity to disarm him.

"I'll need the flashlight," Chase said. "To get my bearings."

The giant tossed it to him. Chase started walking.

"So Malone must be paying you pretty well for this," Chase said, looking over his shoulder.

The giant didn't answer.

"You guys old friends?"

"Shut up."

"You killed a cop. That doesn't go over well here."

The man pushed him from behind. Chase stumbled but managed to stay upright.

"If the price was right, I would kill a hundred of you," the man said. "And Malone has a great deal of money. But my work here is done. After I provide proof that the woman is dead, I will leave your country and no one will ever find me."

Chase had taken forty-three more steps, with the giant close behind him, when he heard the shot. He hit the ground rolling, thinking the man had changed his mind about killing him.

He flipped over just in time to see Raney, her feet planted, her arms extended at shoulder height, fire five more rounds into the giant.

The man fell like a big tree, facedown in the mud.

Raney had never shot a man before. Had never fired a gun. And when it was over, she sank to the ground. Shaking badly.

Chase, sweet Chase, gathered her in his arms. "I've got you. I've got you, Raney," he repeated.

"He hit you," she said. "Your poor head."

"I'm fine. I'm not hurt, honey." He pulled back a little. "I've got to tell you, that scared about five years off my life."

"I know you told me not to get out of the tree."

He laughed. "I don't think I'm going to give you much grief about not following orders."

"I just couldn't wait any longer. I heard the first shot, then two more, and... I thought you'd been shot. And that you might be lying there, bleeding, needing me. I thought about you, the man who always takes care of everybody else. You, the man who never assumes that somebody might care enough to take care of him."

"Raney," he said, his voice sounded strangled.

"I could not stand back and do nothing," she said. "And when I saw him hit you and then do it again, I knew I was going to kill him if I got the chance."

He brushed her hair behind her ears. "Blonde

Raney in action. I love you so much. Whether your hair is blond or brown or Sunset Wonder. I love you. Just you."

She kissed him. "I will love you forever. Now take me home."

* * * * *

Don't miss AGENT BRIDE,
the second book in Beverly Long's miniseries
RETURN TO RAVESVILLE,
on sale wherever Harlequin Intrigue books
and ebooks are sold!

LARGER-PRINT BOOKS!

HARLEQUIN

Presents®

GET 2 FREE LARGER-PRINT NOVELS PLUS 2 FREE GIFTS!

PASSION GUARANTEED SEDUCTION

YES! Please send me 2 FREE LARGER-PRINT Harlequin Presents® novels and my 2 FREE gifts (gifts are worth about $10). After receiving them, if I don't wish to receive any more books, I can return the shipping statement marked "cancel." If I don't cancel, I will receive 6 brand-new novels every month and be billed just $5.30 per book in the U.S. or $5.74 per book in Canada. That's a saving of at least 12% off the cover price! It's quite a bargain! Shipping and handling is just 50¢ per book in the U.S. and 75¢ per book in Canada.* I understand that accepting the 2 free books and gifts places me under no obligation to buy anything. I can always return a shipment and cancel at any time. Even if I never buy another book, the two free books and gifts are mine to keep forever.

176/376 HDN GHVY

Name	(PLEASE PRINT)

Address		Apt. #

City	State/Prov.	Zip/Postal Code

Signature (if under 18, a parent or guardian must sign)

Mail to the **Reader Service:**
IN U.S.A.: P.O. Box 1867, Buffalo, NY 14240-1867
IN CANADA: P.O. Box 609, Fort Erie, Ontario L2A 5X3

**Are you a subscriber to Harlequin Presents® books
and want to receive the larger-print edition?
Call 1-800-873-8635 today or visit us at www.ReaderService.com.**

LARGER-PRINT BOOKS!
GET 2 FREE LARGER-PRINT NOVELS PLUS
2 FREE GIFTS!

HARLEQUIN®

Romance

From the Heart, For the Heart

YES! Please send me 2 FREE LARGER-PRINT Harlequin® Romance novels and my 2 FREE gifts (gifts are worth about $10). After receiving them, if I don't wish to receive any more books, I can return the shipping statement marked "cancel." If I don't cancel, I will receive 4 brand-new novels every month and be billed just $5.09 per book in the U.S. or $5.49 per book in Canada. That's a savings of at least 15% off the cover price! It's quite a bargain! Shipping and handling is just 50¢ per book in the U.S. and 75¢ per book in Canada.* I understand that accepting the 2 free books and gifts places me under no obligation to buy anything. I can always return a shipment and cancel at any time. Even if I never buy another book, the two free books and gifts are mine to keep forever.

119/319 HDN GHWC

Name	(PLEASE PRINT)

Address	Apt. #

City	State/Prov.	Zip/Postal Code

Signature (if under 18, a parent or guardian must sign)

Mail to the **Reader Service:**
IN U.S.A.: P.O. Box 1867, Buffalo, NY 14240-1867
IN CANADA: P.O. Box 609, Fort Erie, Ontario L2A 5X3
Want to try two free books from another line?
Call 1-800-873-8635 or visit www.ReaderService.com.

READERSERVICE.COM

Manage your account online!

- Review your order history
- Manage your payments
- Update your address

> *We've designed the*
> *Reader Service website*
> *just for you.*

Enjoy all the features!

- Discover new series available to you, and read excerpts from any series.
- Respond to mailings and special monthly offers.
- Connect with favorite authors at the blog.
- Browse the Bonus Bucks catalog and online-only exculsives.
- Share your feedback.

Visit us at:
ReaderService.com